THE TESLA CONNECTION

A Cavalier Family Adventure

By Adam Cornell

© Copyright 2012

ISBN: 978-0-9853165-4-9

For Abby, Shaun and Alex

...and for Belinda.

INTRODUCTION
MAY 1891

He hustled across the cobblestone street, dodging the horse-drawn trolley and merging with the foot traffic on 5th Avenue in New York City. The city was alive; the sounds of horse hooves clip-clopping on the street, newspaper hawkers calling out the headlines of the day, and the clacking of shoes on the sidewalk. His course took him by the bakery, and he took a moment to breathe in the delightful fragrance of warm bread baking in the brick ovens. There was no time to dawdle, however, as he carried a very important package under his arm.

He had spent the morning at the glass-maker's shop waiting patiently for the ten glass tubes they needed to complete the machine in the laboratory. The tubes were placed carefully into the special wooden box that they had prepared for the transport. The box had been lined with velvet and spacers to keep the tubes separated and in safe keeping for his seven block walk across the island of Manhattan.

The laboratory was located on the fourth floor of the brick building on Grand Avenue on Manhattan Island in the heart of New York City. As Hudson Cavalier climbed the stairs up to his place of employment, he shifted the package to his other arm and took hold of the railing to aid in his ascent. The smell of tobacco smoke wafted through the building, a fact that irritated Cavalier's employer even as it irritated Hudson's own eyes and nose. As he came to the landing on the fourth floor, he was short of breath, yet happy that his venture had come to an end.

The great Nikola Tesla was busy working on another component of the amazing wireless machine that he promised would revolutionize the world, when Cavalier entered the lab. Tesla did not even look up from his work. He called out to his faithful employee even as he worked on a tiny element of the machine with a small set of steel tools.

"Cavalier! You must complete those tubes by midday if we are to stay on schedule. I plan on working straight on until dawn. We are close, my dear Frenchman. Very close, indeed!"

"Yes, sir," Cavalier said, not looking forward to another night away from his lovely, young wife. As summer was now approaching, he had sent her up to the family estate in the Catskill Mountains, away from the heat of the city. He had hoped he could join her for a few days, having already informed Tesla of this desire for weeks now. Though the man was a genius for all things regarding the universe and its secrets, he seemed baffled by human interaction, budgets and promises to his employees. Hudson was loyal to his employer, but he had to draw the line somewhere. "I was hoping to spend some time with Josephine. Catch a train upstate for a few days."

"Hudson, there will be time for your dalliance with the fairer gender once we have finished assembling the machine. We are so close, can you not taste the electricity in the air?" Tesla had become obsessed with sending energy through the ethos. He had found success the previous year and rather than perfect the apparatus, he had started on an entirely new mechanism. Tesla had worked tirelessly on the new machine and had constructed a monstrosity of glass and metal that stood nearly eight feet tall.

The machine had a large circular grillwork of copper that had been worked to an almost paper thinness. The copper encircled a center node that would release an immense amount of electrical energy. The glass tubes that Cavalier had retrieved from the glassmaker had to be fitted over components that needed to function in a vacuum, that is, without any air. These components were the key to what Tesla hoped to achieve with the machine.

Great steel legs descended from the center of the machine to the floor and were padded with vulcanized rubber mats which separated the machine from the floor. Cavalier had seen all of the elements that had gone into the inner workings of the machine, but he still didn't quite grasp how the machine was meant to work. Tesla's mind worked at such an advanced level than the rest of the men of his era that the depths of his knowledge was practically unfathomable.

Cavalier had already seen amazing things while working for Tesla, and he knew that they were on the cusp of a great breakthrough. He set down the package on his workbench, removed his over coat and hat and donned his work apron and leather gloves that went up to his elbows. He lit the flame of natural gas that would help him heat and shape the glass tubes into the rightly-sized components.

The day dragged on, as Cavalier focused on his work. He completed the necessary work and passed the now properly shaped glass over to Tesla so he could add the circuitry and complete the vacuum tubes. Cavalier now busied himself assisting his employer with the task of sealing the tubes and carefully setting them aside, awaiting installation on the machine.

Just as the sun set in the western sky, the assembly of the machine was completed. Tesla stood back to look at his new masterpiece with pride.

"Tonight will be remembered for all of human history," Tesla said, patting his companion on the shoulder. Tesla was a strikingly tall man with dark hair and mustache, while Cavalier was of modest height and brown, almost blond hair and mustache.

"We should commemorate this moment," Hudson said. "Shall I create a photograph of you in front of your invention?"

"Normally I would scoff at your dramatic suggestion," Tesla said. "But, I believe we owe it to future generations to document this occasion."

Tesla positioned himself in a chair in front of the great machine, and Cavalier readied the large wooden box camera from the Eastman Company. It took several minutes to prepare and stage the photograph, and Tesla began to grow impatient, wanting to get back to his work. Finally the powder flashed and the picture was recorded on the silver plate in the back of the camera.

With that completed, Tesla and Cavalier initiated the startup of the machine. The generator, powered by steam, was brought up to speed by means of stoking the coal fire. Switches were thrown and dials were turned as Nikola Tesla adjusted the apparatus to the desired levels. The copper coils of the large circular grillwork began to spark and glow with energy. A bright light formed at the center and began to widen slowly. The two men stared intently at the phenomenon. Something strange was happening.

"Nikola, do you see?"

"Hush!"

Cavalier could not quite believe his eyes and what they were taking in. The bright light had grown to envelope the entire grillwork now, and great bolts of electricity discharged from the machine to the equipment throughout the laboratory. Tesla walked towards the light, his hand outstretched. He too had seen something in the energy. Hudson grabbed at his employer's arm, but Tesla pulled it away and pressed forward. He reached his hand seemingly right into the energy, going in up to his elbow. Electricity rippled down his body and out to the floor.

Suddenly there was a violent burst of energy, and Tesla was thrown across the laboratory. The machine gave off a second bright burst and then went dark. The room fell silent. The sun had set outside and the burst of energy had blown out the gaslights throughout the lab. Additionally, the room was now filled with smoke as Cavalier realized that the machine had caught fire. He was quick with the sand buckets to extinguish the flames. Once he was sure there was no further danger from the fire, he opened the large windows to let out the smoke.

As the room cleared, Tesla and Cavalier surveyed the equipment. Neither of the men could believe what they saw before them.

"Impossible," Cavalier said.

CHAPTER 1
PRESENT DAY

"But I don't want to go," Tipp Cavalier said crossing his arms. There was a weekend home stand by the Mets and he always got to go to the weekend games. Also there was an exhibit on Harry Houdini that was just opening in Midtown Manhattan. There was no way he was missing that! He stood on the sidewalk outside their brownstone apartment in Brooklyn Heights, New York, watching his parents load luggage into the cab. His arms were folded sternly across his chest, and he stomped a sneakered foot for emphasis. He was a bright boy for eight years old, but he was also quite stubborn. His father called him a handful. His mother called him precocious. His sister called him a royal pain. But even she agreed with him every once in awhile.

"Me, neither," Elina, Tipp's sister, echoed. She also had big plans for the weekend and none of them included being kidnapped by her own parents and taken to stay with family upstate. They hadn't been given any information about the nature of this unplanned interruption of their young lives. Their parents had merely told them to get packed, as they were going to stay with Great Grandpa Dickie. The announcement regarding the trip from their apartment in the city to their great-grandfather's enormous mansion on the island near Watertown, NY had come with far too short a notice for her liking. Elina preferred plenty of time for preparation for such an excursion. She needed that time to pack all of her necessities and even some of the not-so-necessities. There had been barely enough time to accomplish the feat.

Though the packing was done, she still would have preferred just a few more hours to make sure that the outfits she had selected were appropriate. She'd stalled as much as she could until she had to be practically dragged out the door. Elina was about to raise another complaint, but she could read the facial expressions of her parents. Something was troubling them. So, she stifled her grievance and kept it to herself. Her father and mother were making quiet comments to each other as they loaded the bags, and they were moving quickly. They had already filled one cab full and it was on its way to the train station ahead of them. Peter had sent along their housekeeper, Mrs. Backnackerson, to arrange transferring the luggage from the cab to the train car.

"What's wrong?" Elina Cavalier asked her mother, Asta. "Why are you packing so much stuff?"

"We will tell you on the way. Right now, we just need to hurry and get to Penn Station," Asta replied, as she lifted the last bag into the hatchback of the minivan cab. Elina reluctantly climbed into the cab while her brother stood like a stubborn statue on the sidewalk. Peter didn't have time for discussion. He scooped his son up and placed him into the cab, slid the door closed, and then climbed into the front seat. They were off.

"We're taking the train up to Syracuse. Great Grandpa Dickie's driver will be there to pick you up and take you on up to the house. Then, Mom and I have to take the train over to Chicago to catch a flight," He said over his shoulder to them as the cab traveled across the Brooklyn Bridge into Manhattan. Peter's tone was serious, and both Tipp and Elina took note. Their father was usually carefree and joking. He was a teaser and he loved playing pranks. At first, the children had believed this to be another one of his pranks, albeit an extremely elaborate one. But, the clues began to pile up, indicating that something extremely unusual was afoot. First, the phone calls in the middle of the night. Then, the quiet conversations their parents had which would drop to silence whenever either of the children entered the room. A phone call in the dead of night had gotten Peter and Asta packing and, as soon as the children had awoken, they were pressed into packing for themselves, though Mrs. Backnackerson had helped quite a bit. Additionally, the bags that their parents had brought were not the normal vacation bags they were used to. The children had seen back packs and climbing gear, ice axes and winter parkas, all getting packed into the taxi. Something was definitely going on.

After the detail-free explanation from their father, the children rode in silence, watching the great city of New York slide by. They had taken this trip for many summers previous, heading north up the island of Manhattan toward Penn Station. They would get their boarding passes, board the train, ride along the Hudson River, turn west at Albany, head across New York State to Syracuse and then get off the train and into a car for the automotive leg of the journey to great-grandfather's house. This time, though, unlike previous trips, their parents wouldn't be joining them.

Her parents had told her to pack light and to do so quickly, so Elina only had ten separate outfits which could all be mixed and matched. By her calculations she had exactly one hundred and twelve different combinations, not including underwear or jacket. She also packed all of her personal toiletries; toothbrush, hairbrush, shampoo, conditioner, deodorant, face cream, and moisturizer. Her nail kit was also neatly stowed away in the full size suitcase which was now too heavy for anyone but her father to carry.

"I'm glad this thing has wheels," Peter said as he lugged her bag through Penn Station towards the train. "What did you pack in this thing, bricks or lead bars?" Mrs. Backnackerson had hired a man with a cart to take the first load down to the train when she had arrived ahead of them in the first taxi. With that luggage stowed, she was patiently waiting for them with another man and another cart when their cab pulled up. Everything fit onto the cart except, of course, Elina's bag. So Peter was forced to drag it behind him as they snaked through the crowd towards their platform.

"Only the important stuff, Dad," Elina answered as she followed their course via the map program on her tablet computer. She felt the need to always know where they were and where they were going. On family trips she would trace their progress along interstate highways or from port to port when they took the yacht. She hadn't taken the train since she'd owned it. So, despite her initial reluctance, she was beginning to foster a small level of excitement to challenge herself to trace their progress along the rail line up the Hudson River

She had received the computer tablet as a gift for a good report card, and used it constantly. It was filled with videos, music, maps, books, encyclopedias, dictionaries, a litany of games, applications of all sorts, and of course, the ability to connect to the internet.

Unlike his sister, Tipp had indeed packed lightly with exactly one alternate pair of pants, one t-shirt, one change of underwear and one change of socks. The rest of his bag was filled with a book on baseball, his baseball glove, his game console with fourteen different games, and his most treasured possession in all the world: a Harry Houdini Escape Artist's set.

He had received the set as a gift from his father after they went to see a stage show in Las Vegas the previous autumn. The illusionist did some of the standard tricks like levitation and sawing a woman in half, but the submerged man act was what really caught Tipp's attention. The illusionist was chained and locked tight. An audience member even checked the locks to make sure. He was then lowered into a tank filled with water. The lid was then shut and locked. The illusionist set to freeing himself using picks and such, while a digital clock ticked away above him. After two minutes he'd freed himself from the chains and then stuck his hands through holes in the top of the tank lid to work on the exterior lock of the tank. After three minutes the illusionist was free, gasping for air, all to the uproarious applause of the audience, who could move back from the edges of their seats and use their hands for something other than gripping the armrests of their chairs.

Tipp had tried to hold his breath for as long as the illusionist was remained immersed, but he gave out less than a minute into the act. It wasn't the fact that the man could hold his breath for so long that especially impressed Tipp. It was that the escapist could open locks without keys. He could trick the locks into thinking that the keys were being used and they would give up and open. To Tipp it was as if the escapist had found a way to reason with the very laws of physics, to have a conversation with those laws and win the argument! Tipp wanted to learn how.

In the gift shop, after the show, his father pointed out a book about Harry Houdini, the greatest escape artist of all time. And there, right next to the book, was an official lock picking set. Tipp begged for both the book and the set, but they left the gift shop without either. Tipp was certainly disappointed. However he had been taught that he didn't always get what he wanted, even if the family was quite wealthy. Three weeks later, upon returning from classes, Tipp found a neatly wrapped box lying on his bed. He tore into the brightly colored paper to find both the book and the Official Harry Houdini Escape Artist's set. The set came with a warning that it was intended for entertainment purposes only and not to be used for criminal activity. It didn't say anything about mischievousness.

The set included a leather wallet with several lock picks and torsion wrenches. Within weeks he quickly became quite adept at using the set, and soon there wasn't a lock in their entire building that he wasn't able to pick. Though he regretted not getting to see the Mets take on the Giants, or being there for the new Houdini exhibit, he didn't view the weekend as a complete loss. He was excited to try his skills on all of the old fashioned locks in Great Grandpa Dickie's mansion.

So, like his sister, Tipp had adapted quickly to the new plans that had been foisted upon them. For their own, quite dissimilar, reasons, in the short time since they had started out on their trip, both children had found something to be excited about. Neither would let their parents know it, of course.

ADAM CORNELL

CHAPTER 2

The family pushed through the pedestrian traffic of the busy Penn Station and down to platform number six. They would be riding the Empire Line out of New York City, along the Hudson River, stopping in Syracuse. The children would depart the train there, meet up with the awaiting limo driver, while Asta and Peter would continue on to Chicago where their private jet was waiting. There was just one thing the children didn't know: Why?

The whispers and secret conversations had started two days earlier, and had become more frequent and more intense with each passing day. There was something terribly wrong; something so wrong that both Peter and Asta were planning a flight to Antarctica. It was either Antarctica or Alaska, or maybe Arkansas. Tipp couldn't be positive about the location he'd overheard his parents discussing. He kept trying to creep into the room while they were talking in hushed tones to solve the mystery, but they always seemed to know when he was there, as if they sensed it, and they would cease the conversation or pretend like they were talking about something else. He was ninety-nine percent sure they had said Antarctica. Elina didn't believe him.

The family traveled along the length of the train on the platform and followed the direction of the conductor as he showed them to their car. Peter had called ahead and arranged for the family's private railcar to be adjoined to the train just ahead of the dining car. It made for a much more comfortable on long trips.

"Money can't buy happiness," Peter would lecture time and time again. "At best it can buy comfort and a level of security. But even those can be short-lived." Even so, being able to ride in their own private railcar was pretty sweet.

The car was a deep maroon color with gold accents and deeply tinted windows. It had a name on the side in beautiful gold leaf lettering: Josephine. The children had traveled on the special car before, but still found it fascinating and beautiful. It had been in the family for generations. Peter had commissioned its interior rebuilt two years earlier to have all of the modern conveniences. It was the best way to travel the country.

Their baggage was quickly placed in the appropriate storage compartments, and they each found a seat and tried to get comfortable. Peter didn't even have a moment to exhale before the questions started.

"Where are you going?"

"What's going on?"

"Is somebody in trouble?"

"Why are you going to Antarctica?"

"Is it really Antarctica or is it Arkansas?"

"What's in Arkansas?"

"Settle down!" Peter raised his voice above the children's to get their attention. "I will tell you what happened, but you must calm down first." Peter cleared his throat, looked to Asta, and was met with a reassuring nod. He began to tell them what had happened to the children's grandparents.

"You know how we've told you that Grandpa Clive and Grandma Kaye are important scientists? Well, they have been working on a top secret project for the U.S. government down in Antarctica.

"See, I told you," Tipp said to his sister.

"Whatever," she replied.

"They were taking a break from their work for a two week vacation in Australia when they were kidnapped," Peter continued.

"What?!"

"Who did it?"

"Are they okay?"

"Will we ever see them again?"

"Calm down, calm down," Peter said. The children had frightened looks on their faces. He extended his arms to them and they both ran over and climbed up onto his lap. He was a large man, standing nearly six and a half feet tall, which meant when he was sitting, he had plenty of lap for both of them. "Your mother and I are flying down to Australia to help with the investigation. The authorities believe that the kidnapping has something to do with their research. We think they will be just fine, but we have to find them, and fast. Now, I don't have any more details to give you, but you both can be sure that we will do all we can to get your Grandma and Grandpa back safely. We will spare no expense. In the meantime, you two have to be extra, special good for your Great Grandpa Dickie. He's getting up there in years now and can't be chasing you all over the house."

"Pfft, we're not allowed all over the house," Tipp said with a sour disposition. "He makes us stay either in our rooms or in the kitchen. No fooling about!" Tipp tried to do an impression of how his Great-grandfather spoke and twitched his head back and forth for emphasis while wagging a finger at his sister. This made Elina giggle, but then she remembered the seriousness of what was going on and stopped herself.

"But, what if they're not okay? What if the people who took them try to hurt them or," Elina didn't want to say what she was thinking out loud. "Worse," she finished, gulping as the word came out.

"Well, we're going to do everything we can to make sure that nothing like that happens," Asta said bravely. "It's a dangerous world out there, especially for people like us who have money. There are always criminals who think it would just be easier to steal our money than to work hard for their own."

"Anyway, we don't think this is about money," Peter said. "The police in Australia are under the impression, and our intelligence agencies here agree, that the special secret project they were working on is the reason for their disappearance. If that's true, then it's probably another government that's responsible for the kidnapping, and they wouldn't dare hurt them for fear of retaliation from our government. Your Grandma and Grandpa are very well connected in Washington, D.C."

"I hope they will be okay," Elina said as she put her head down on her father's shoulder.

"I hope so too, sweetpea," Peter replied. "Perhaps, we can say a little prayer together for their safety."

The family prayed for the safe return of Grandma and Grandpa Cavalier as the train rumbled up the Hudson River Line. Slowly, the city faded behind them and the beautiful countryside rose up on each side of the Hudson River. Lush green foliage in the trees, bright blue sky with puffy white clouds and the warm sunshine made for an inviting and idyllic scene. The trees whipped passed their windows in a blur of greenery. Out on the river, a few boaters were taking advantage of the warm, late spring day, hoisting multi-colored sails to catch the light wind. To the children, it seemed so strange to have such a beautiful day outside while their moods were so gloomy inside.

The car was laid out like a small home. A sitting area stretched across the entire width of the car with large picture windows on each side for gazing at the passing scenery. A small, well stocked snack area was in the center of the car and separated the sitting area from the bedrooms. They would take their meals in the dining car along with the other passengers of the train, but it was always nice to have some snacks. From the snack bar a narrow corridor led back along the center of the magnificent car, with two bunk rooms on each side.

The bunk rooms were private riding compartments that could be transformed from a sitting room into bunk beds. When they were in riding mode, they featured two cushioned chairs facing each other with a table in the center. To convert into a bedroom, a porter would lower the table, roll the seats toward each other and then pull down a comfortable mattress which would accordion out from the wall. A bunk also folded down from above the window. The children would, on occasion, be allowed to invite some of their friends along on family excursions, and the extra beds came in handy.

The master bedroom took up all but a narrow passageway of the railcar's width. It featured a California king-sized bed, which was a bit longer than a standard king-sized bed, a flat screen TV which was connected to a satellite on the railcar's roof and a Blu-ray player. Peter had also brought along his video game system on the last trip. The kids weren't the only ones that enjoyed video games in the Cavalier family.

The children wouldn't be spending the night on the train, so the bunks were up and they had their choice of the private sitting rooms or the main room. Normally, they rushed into the car to choose their room for the duration of the ride, but this time they preferred to be with their parents.

After, several stops along the way and nearly five hours of travel, the train pulled into the Syracuse rail station. The children were hustled out the door into the welcoming arms of Sullivan O'Grady, the chief caretaker of the vast Cavalier estate in the Thousand Islands region. He was Great Grandpa Dickie's right hand man and could be trusted to guard the children's lives with his own. He was an enormous man, making their own father seem rather ordinary in comparison. He had no children of his own, and therefore had a special fondness for the great-grandchildren of his boss. And the children absolutely adored him.

"Sullo!" They both cried out his nickname as they ran towards him. He scooped them both up as if they weighed the same as two feathers and swung them up onto his shoulders. They waved to their parents from their perch atop the giant as the train began to pull out of the station. Both of the children had a feeling of dread as they realized that their parents were about to embark on a very dangerous journey around the world to try to locate their missing grandparents. They didn't want to stay behind but, they were old enough to know that it was the right thing to do.

After the train disappeared around the bend, Sullo set the children down and snatched up their bags. He had a deep baritone voice and an absolutely amazing red, handlebar mustache. He had no hair on the rest of his head and wore his driver's cap so as to cover it up. He looked like one of those old-timey boxers that peppered the pages of some of the old books that Tipp loved to read. His exterior seemed intimidating, but inside was a heart of pure gold.

Sullo had driven the limousine, which meant that the children got to ride in the back and watch a movie for the rest of the two hour drive up to their great-grandfather's house. Sullo laid out an array of different snacks and drinks for their enjoyment, and contented himself glancing back in his rear view mirror every few moments to see the children happily munching away and enjoying the film.

Finally, just after three in the afternoon, the limousine arrived at the large steel gates of the Cavalier estate in Clayton, New York. Large letter C's decorated the ornate ironwork of the gates which swung open automatically as the car approached. The driveway wound down away from the road to a small house on the shore. Within the small house was a boat which would take them out to the privately owned island.

Sullo fit each of the children with a life vest and loaded the luggage into the boat. It roared to life and he slowly backed it away from the dock. They taxied away from shore, and as they cleared the no-wake zone, Sullo pushed the throttle to the stops and the boat leapt forward. The nose lifted from the water even as a foaming white wake trailed behind them. The children screamed with joy, squinting against the wind and water spray. There weren't too many kids who got to ride a train, limo, and boat to get to their great-grandfather's house. They knew they were probably the luckiest kids in the world.

Sullo had barely pulled the boat to the dock before the children had sprung from their seats and were rushing up the wooden planks towards shore. Great Grandpa Dickie slowly came down the marble steps of the great house and met the children half way. They showered him with hugs and kisses. He had taken to walking with a cane now, and he dropped it to the ground with a clatter as he received the children into his arms. The embrace was long and loving. He was well aware that his son and daughter-in-law had gone missing and that it was up to his grandson and grand-daughter-in-law to rescue them. He was also aware of a great many other things that threatened the family. Things that none of them could imagine. He had held onto those secrets for a very long time.

"Come inside children, I am so excited to have you here," he said, as he bent over to retrieve his cane, letting out a grunt as he did so. "You are going to have the experience of a lifetime!"

Sullo brought the bags and took them up the stairs to the children's rooms. They would be staying indefinitely, so he had prepared a room for each of them just down the hall from their great-grandfather's. He watched the old man walk slowly behind the children as they went into the sitting room. He was up to something, but Sullo wasn't sure what it was. Whatever the crazy, old rascal had hatched up, it would be good. The unmistakable gleam of adventure had returned to the old man's eyes.

CHAPTER 3

Great Grandpa Dickie sat in his large, high-backed leather chair which faced the enormous television. For the moment the television was off, as it was still too early for a baseball game. He held in his hand a picture that he looked at with a dreamy, far off gaze. The children were sitting crisscross-applesauce (they didn't call it Indian-style anymore) on the floor in front of him. They were waiting for him to start speaking. He always had the most amazing stories for them. Now, however, he just sat looking at the picture, and Elina could swear that tears were forming in the corners of his bright blue eyes.

"Children. Elina and Tipp. My only great-grand children. What I'm about to tell you may scare you, but it's important that you both be brave," he said with a heavy sigh. "I'm going to die sometime this weekend."

"What?"

"No, you're not!"

"You can't!"

"We need to go to the hospital!"

"Children, listen to me. Please," he said as both Elina and Tipp started to cry. He realized they were so young, but this was the time. All of the events had fallen into place and he knew what the culmination of those events would be.

"Calm down. We still have some time. I'm sure of it. So let's make it the best we've ever had. Once I'm gone, you two will have full run of the house. Anyplace you want to go, any door you wish to open, you're free to do so."

"But we don't want you to die!" Elina cried.

"If we're good, can you stay longer?" Tipp said between sniffles.

"Children, it is just my time to go. Death is indeed an enemy and someday it will be conquered. But for now, it's a reality and a part of life. I've lived a good long time. Some might say longer than I have any right to. Well those people would be wrong! Nobody wants to die, and I certainly don't. But I have it on good authority that my time has come. I'm not going to focus on the negative, though! I've been blessed to see my children grow and have children of their own, and then those children have you two. It's been a true blessing. I've also seen and experienced many things that most people would call too fantastic to be real. I've recorded many of those experiences in the books within the library. Now that you're old enough, you'll be able to read and understand that the world you live in is not as it appears. There are a great many mysteries that you will uncover and I will be along for the ride through my books. You'll never feel like I'm not with you."

It was just too much for the children to bear any longer. They both leapt to their feet and hugged their great-grandfather, weeping as they did so. Tears were also streaming down the old man's withered cheeks. After a few moments, he pushed them back so he could look them in the eyes.

"That's enough crying, don't you think? We haven't much time, so let's go have some fun! What do you say?"

"Ya!" The children chorused, still sniffing.

They went out to the big toy garage, as Great Grandpa Dickie called it, and each of them donned a helmet. Three off-road, motorized racing carts sat on the polished concrete floor of the garage, prepped and ready to go. One was painted pink, the other blue, the last bright green.

"I get the pink one!" Elina yelled as she put on her helmet and let her great grandfather buckle the strap under her chin. Tipp chose the blue one, leaving the green cart for Great Grandpa Dickie.

The engines started with a flick of a switch, and they revved the motors as the large garage door was opened by Sullo. Tipp was the first out, mashing the accelerator to the floor and leaving twin patches of burnt rubber on the concrete floor. Elina was after him moments later, with their great-grandfather tailing them.

The children had been trained to drive this style of off-road carts the previous summer, and loved following the trails across the family property. It was a large island, so there were plenty of trails crisscrossing it, promising hours of high-speed fun.

The carts featured spring suspension, knobby tires for

gripping the dirt, a five-point seatbelt harness system, a sturdy roll cage, and loud horns that the children took to using almost as soon as they discovered them.

The three of them went tearing up the hill, through the apple and pear trees, heading for the trails that snaked between the trees of the woods. Even though it was an island, there were plenty of animals on it. In the winter, if it got cold enough, the water would freeze and allow animals easy access to the islands to find new homes. Over the previous winter, a family of white-tailed deer had come to Cavalier Island, and they could be seen in the mornings eating grass at the edge of the woods.

Tipp was still in the lead as they entered the woods, tearing down the dirt roads that had been cleared for both the carts in the summer and snowmobiles in the winter. Their great-grandfather had always made sure there were activities to do outside. There were horses, the off-road carts, and even a grand 1/8th scale steam train that followed tracks around the property. Elina remembered riding the train when she was still just a little girl, and thinking that it was the best thing in the entire world.

The strange thing about their great-grandfather was that he never let them explore the interior of the house. They had the run of the entire property and had probably walked every inch of the island, except for the hallways and rooms of the enormous mansion. The doors were locked, and whenever either of them had tried to venture off on their own, either Great Grandpa Dickie or Sullo was right there to stop them. It was frustrating to the likes of two very curious children like Elina and Tipp, but, soon after they would always lose themselves in the planned activities their great-grandfather had for them.

The three of them spent nearly an hour flying through the woods with engines roaring and mud flying. Their helmets were equipped with a communications system, so they could talk with each other as they drove. Mostly the wireless sound waves were littered with just whoops of joy and cheers of sheer glee. The children were having so much fun, they had almost completely forgotten that their great-grandfather had told them of his assured imminent demise.

Great Grandpa Dickie finally took the lead on a wide corner and told the children over their headsets to follow him, there was a surprise he wanted to show them. They headed down a path that neither of the children remembered ever seeing before. They weren't sure if it was new or if they had merely missed it before, though they couldn't imagine how. They went over a bit of a crest at great speed and they felt the wheels leave the earth for a moment. It made their stomachs drop. The both of them loved it when that happened.

Finally their great-grandfather stopped in a clearing and turned off his engine. It was a grassy area beneath an opening in the trees. At one end of the clearing, opposite the path from which they'd entered, there was a concrete building that seemed to go into the solid rock behind it. A great steel door blocked entry to the building.

ADAM CORNELL

Great Grandpa Dickie unbuckled his seatbelt restraints and removed his helmet. His white hair stood straight up on his head and reminded the children of one of those troll dolls. He took a moment to let the sun shine onto his face. It was as if he was drinking it for the last time. Elina thought for a moment that maybe that was exactly what he was doing. The children extracted themselves from their carts as well and followed their great-grandfather over to the steel door.

"Take a look," he said to them as he pressed his hand against the concrete and a panel popped open. Behind the fake concrete panel was a keypad. "One. Eight. Nine. One."

Suddenly the steel door rumbled to life and slid open.

"Remember that number," he said to the children. "Eighteen-ninety-one. Repeat it."

"Eighteen-ninety-one," the children echoed.

"You won't have any trouble remembering it, I promise you. Eighteen-ninety-one," he repeated. He pulled the steel door closed and the children heard loud clanking as it locked shut.

"We're not going in?" Tipp asked.

"No, not now. You will soon enough, but now isn't the right time. When the family is back together and you're a bit older, you'll need to find shelter here. It will protect you from even the worst of disasters."

"Great Grandpa Dickie, what are you talking about? Is there going to be a disaster?" Elina asked.

"Oh, maybe. It's just an old man trying to protect his progeny. Don't worry about it now. I just wanted to show it to you," he said.

"What's a progeny?" Tipp asked.

"My offspring. Descendants. You. You're my progeny. All I want to do is protect you two. You have no idea how important you are," he said.

"I think we should get back to the house and get some water to drink," Elina said. "And maybe an aspirin." Her great-grandfather wasn't making much sense. She was worried he was starting to lose it. It would be better if they all got back to the house as quickly as possible so Sullo would be around to help if something bad happened.

They buckled back into their carts and headed back to the house. They didn't go quite as fast and there wasn't as much whooping and cheering. A dark cloud had come over them. Elina didn't like the way their great-grandfather was talking, and it scared her. She didn't know if Tipp was picking up on it, but Great Grandpa Dickie was making preparations for his death. Showing them the emergency shelter was a big clue that he was serious about it.

When they returned and had parked the carts, the children found their way into the house and cleaned up in their individual bathrooms. They were covered from head to toe with mud, grass, gravel and leaves from their "extreme racing adventure of extreme racing fun," as Tipp called it in his best Monster-Truck-Announcer's voice.

When they were done cleaning up, they went back to

the sitting room and found Great Grandpa Dickie tidied up as well, sitting in his high-backed chair, staring at the picture he had held earlier. When the children entered the room, he placed the photo face down on the table next to him.

"How about some food?" he said, pulling himself slowly to his feet. In Elina's eyes, he seemed to have gotten progressively older and weaker since they had arrived, even since they had finished riding the racing carts. He strained to get out of the chair and walk with them towards the great kitchen where Alonzo, the chef, was preparing lunch.

The three of them ate in relative silence. Elina kept stealing glances at her great-grandfather, as each bite seemed to be a labor. Tipp was completely unaware. After they'd finished lunch, Great Grandpa Dickie walked slowly back to the sitting room.

"I'm going to go lay down," he said. "You two can stay in here and play video games if you'd like. Don't worry, I'm just going to rest for a bit. I love you both very, very much. I'm proud of you both. Always remember who you are. You're Cavaliers."

It was an odd thing to say and only increased Elina's growing angst. Tipp seemed oblivious as he ran over to open the cabinet where the video game systems were, before grabbing a controller. As the game powered up, Elina came over and sat beside him. She wasn't in the mood to play.

"Do you think Great Grandpa Dickie is really going to die this weekend," she asked her brother. He was two and a half years younger than her and was a boy, so she wasn't sure if he was mature enough to understand what was going on.

"I don't know," Tipp said. "I don't want to think about it."

"I can't stop thinking about it," she said, standing. She went over to her great-grandfather's chair and sat down, watching her brother play a game that involved trying to collect as many jewels as possible while bopping bad guys on the head with a spin jump. The game which so engrossed Tipp, bored her to death, so she soon found herself drifting off to sleep. She lazily rolled her head back and forth against the chair back, not really sure if she wanted to take a nap or find something else to do. Her eyes landed on the picture frame that her great-grandfather had been looking at, and she reached over to pick it up. At first, what she saw didn't make sense. She looked closer and closer.

"Tipp," she said. He was perfecting spin jumps that caused the bad guys to crumble into a pile of robot parts. He didn't reply. "Tipp! Look at this."

"What? I'm busy," he said.

"You have to look at this picture. Pause the game!" she insisted. She brought it over to him and stuck it in front of his face. This forced him to pause the game.

"What?" he barked at her with irritation. Video games always made him irritable, which is why when he was home there were strict limits on how much time he could play.

"What is it?" he continued, looking at the picture but not understanding.

"This picture, look at it," she said. "Look at the kids!"

It took a moment for it to sink in, but then she saw recognition and understanding sweep across his freckled features.

"It's us!" he exclaimed finally.

"Yes, it's us. I don't remember taking this picture, do you?" She asked.

"No. Who is that with us? It looks like a younger version of Great Grandpa Dickie," Tipp said.

The picture was of a young man, perhaps in his early twenties, standing next to a great machine with two children that looked exactly like Tipp and Elina. They were dressed in clothes that looked like they were from a century ago; like they were dressed up for an old movie or something. The man that looked like a younger version of their great-grandfather wore a bowler hat and a suit, while the girl that looked like Elina was in a long dress. The dress could have been worn in a Broadway musical or something. The boy who looked like Tipp had a suit very similar to the Great Grandpa Dickie lookalike, but with a cabbie hat. The photo was black and white, though it had now browned and faded quite a bit. The more Elina looked at it, she was sure that the children were the two of them.

"Look! Those are my boots!" Elina said. She held out her feet to show her brother. Sure enough, the girl in the photo wore boots similar to Elina's. They were the popular pull on leather style with the fleece interiors.

"Pfft," Tipp made a noise with his mouth. "They're just moccasins. Look."

Elina looked at the picture closely. She had to agree, they did look like Native American leather boots. She couldn't see the boy's shoes, as there was a shadow across his feet and it made it difficult to see.

She pried off the back of the frame and carefully slid the photo out. On the back there was writing in a neat and legible script:

Elina, Tipp and Hudson, May 30, 1891.

"Oh. Em. Gee," Elina said. "Tipp look at this." She showed him the writing and he scrunched up his face in confusion.

"It doesn't make sense," he said.

Just then, Sullo walked into the room. His eyes were red and his great handlebar mustache was drooping down on both sides of his mouth, wet with tears.

"Children," he said with a quivering voice. "Your great-grandfather has just passed away."

CHAPTER 4

The children sat quietly as Sullo spoke with the sheriff's deputy who had traveled out to the island by boat. Sullo was explaining how he had gone up to check on the old man and found him unconscious on the floor and not breathing. He'd never made it to his nap. The kids had cried their eyes out already, and were now in disbelief that he was really gone. He had always seemed so full of life to them, always planning some big adventure. It was like he was a kid just like them. He couldn't be dead.

"How are you two holding up?" Sheriff's Deputy Brent Shelley asked.

"Okay," Elina gulped out. Tipp didn't reply at all. He just leaned against his older sister who put her arm around him. "I just can't believe he's gone."

"I know, he was a cool old guy," the deputy said. "It was his time. I'm sorry. He was ninety-one years old. He didn't look a day over seventy, though. There's something else I need to talk to you two about. We can't get a hold of your parents on the phone."

"They're flying to Australia to look for my grandparents who have been kidnapped because they're top secret scientists," Elina said.

"Oh. I see," the deputy said, though Elina could tell he didn't believe her. "Well I know Sullo here is a trusted family friend. For now, I'm going to leave you in his custody until we can reach your parents. Are you both okay with that?"

"Yeah. Sullo will take care of us," Elina said. Tipp still didn't say anything.

"What about you?" the chief asked. Elina gave her brother a nudge to get a response.

"Yeah," he said sullenly. "Sullo will take care of us. He's good."

"Okay. Well, Sullivan, I'll be in touch. Thanks." Deputy Shelley shook Sullo's hand and then left. Once he was gone, the children ran to Sullo and hugged him, crying with grief. The big man wept with them. Great Grandpa Dickie Cavalier was gone.

It had been two days since the children had lost their great-grandfather. They still hadn't been able to track down their parents. Sullo had called the airport in Chicago and had acquired the flight plan which was filed by their pilot. He was able to track the flight from Chicago to Los Angeles. From there the flight plan called for a stop for a refueling stop in Honolulu, Hawaii, then a straight shot to Australia. Usually, on long trips, they would be available by satellite phone, but they weren't picking up. They should have landed in Australia by now, as each airport had reported that they had been on schedule. It was a surprise to both children that their parents hadn't bothered to call and check in. It was certainly not like them.

The skies were dark and gloomy and it had begun raining early in the morning, so the children couldn't go outside and play. They were in the sitting room, Tipp playing video games half-heartedly while Elina read a book on her computer tablet.

"I miss Mom and Dad," Tipp said, shutting off the game console and returning the wireless controller to the charging station.

"Me too," Elina said looking up from her tablet. "I wish they would come home."

"I'm bored," Tipp said.

"Me too," Elina said.

"Let's go explore the house."

"We shouldn't."

"Why not? Great Grandpa Dickie said we could, once he was gone, remember?"

"Yeah, but we shouldn't mess anything up. Mom and Dad would be mad."

"Well, I'm going," Tipp said, heading out of the room.

"Wait for me," Elina said, grabbing her tablet case with the shoulder strap. She slid the computer tablet into the case and then slung the strap over her head and across her body. She followed her brother out into the vast house.

ADAM CORNELL

The house had seventeen rooms not counting the confusing maze of storage rooms in the cellar. In the entryway was the great staircase which climbed up twelve steps to a landing and then, split to the right and the left for another ten steps. The house was divided into two wings from the staircase, with four bedrooms and two bathrooms in each of the upstairs wings. The children usually stayed in the east wing, as they both liked to awaken to the sunshine. The large kitchen was on the first floor in the west wing, while the sitting room and study were in the east wing. Under the staircase, beneath large wooden arches, was the entrance into the enormous library. Three additional bathrooms were scattered throughout the first floor layout.

Of all the rooms in the house, the library was the one room that the children were most curious about and yet had received little or no access to. Both of them had a love for books along with an innate passion for reading. Elina had already read many of the classics, whereas Tipp would lose himself in non-fiction books about Harry Houdini or the Titanic or the 1928 New York Yankees. They had only been allowed in the library once. It had been several years ago, but if their memories served them correctly, what they saw when they opened the doors to the enormous room, appeared exactly as they had recalled. Nothing seemed to have moved at all. The books all seemed in the same places, the furniture all neatly arranged as it was the last time they had been allowed a quick peek. It was as if the room had been in a time capsule, so protective had their great-grandfather been of his library.

It was a vast, circular room, nearly forty feet wide and rising two full stories. The walls were lined with shelves and shelves of books; a veritable silo of knowledge. A huge open atrium of a room, though the ceiling didn't have glass. Large marble columns rose, in what might be considered, the corners of the room, though the walls circled behind the columns continuing the room's circumference. The columns reached to the ceiling, which stretched over in an amazing dome that gave the sensation of gazing up into the outdoors, though it was as solid as the walls. The domed ceiling was painted to only look like the sky with clouds in it. The most amazing thing was that the painting had been done in such a way and the lighting had been positioned such that, when they were dimmed, the lights could portray the effect of a bright blue midday sky with puffy white clouds, a purple and red dusk with orange clouds, or a violet night sky with twinkling stars. It was absolutely gorgeous. Tipp lost himself for several minutes just playing with the light switch.

The second floor could be reached by a spiral staircase. It led up to an ornate iron catwalk which circled the entire room. There were literally thousands of books dating back to before the house was even built. They were both quiet as they took in the vastness of the cathedral-like place.

"It smells like Great Grandpa in here," Tipp said, his hushed voice somehow echoing around the chamber.

"Yeah, it does," Elina replied quietly. The room featured leather, upholstered chairs and a couch as well as a wet bar with all sorts of fancy bottles filled with many different colored liquids. A fireplace was at the far end of the room, opposite the entryway. Tall windows stretched up on each side of the fireplace nearly to the ceiling, and they looked out onto the back garden.

Something immediately caught Elina's attention. It was a yellowed envelope. The curious envelope sat on a wooden stand between the two high-backed, leather chairs which were facing the fireplace. The envelope was propped up, as if it was being presented to her. As she drew closer, she saw the words that were hand written on the outside of it: To Tipp and Elina Cavalier.

"Hey, Tipp. Look at this!" Elina rushed over and grabbed the envelope from the stand and showed the outside to her brother.

"What is it?"

"I don't know," Elina answered. "I just found it."

"Let me see it," Tipp grabbed for it, but his older sister was too quick. She pulled it out of his grasp and started to open it. He wasn't going to give up that easily. He grabbed at it again, and once again she pulled it away.

"Give it to me!" Tipp yelled and pounced on his sister. She screamed and fought him off. They fell to the floor, wrestling for the envelope. Elina kept it just out of his grasp with Tipp trying ever more earnestly to grab it. Finally, Tipp grabbed hold, and this time when Elina tugged it away, the envelope ripped right down the middle. A yellowed piece of paper fluttered to the ground.

"You ripped it!" Elina bellowed, as she leapt for the

letter that had fallen free. She didn't wait for Tipp to make an attempt to grab at that. She ran for the spiral staircase and raced up to the second level. She knew her brother was afraid of heights and wouldn't follow her.

"No fair!" He yelled after her. He sat on the second step of the staircase and planted his chin firmly into his hands with a huff.

Elina opened the letter carefully, as she realized how old it was now. She read the whole thing through, from beginning to end, but it didn't make any sense to her. She read it again, but was still baffled.

"Tipp, this letter doesn't make any sense," she called out to him from the steel catwalk above him. She was sitting on the floor, dangling her legs over the edge and leaning on the railing.

"Who cares!" Tipp called back to her.

"No, listen! It's addressed to you and me!" Elina continued.

"What does it say?"

"Here, I'll read it to you!" Elina said.

"I can read it by myself! I'm not a baby!"

"Will you just be quiet for a second and listen!" Elina said. She cleared her throat and began to read the letter to her younger brother. He let out a grunt and sat with his elbows on his knees and his chin in his hands.

"Dearest Tipp and Elina, It has now been several weeks since your fantastic departure. There are some nights, as I sit with my work, that I wonder if you were even real or just a figment of my overactive imagination. I need but look around to see the clues of your reality and even then, I can't believe it. I know not if you will ever read this, but if so, know that I care for you both very deeply and will never forget all that you have done for both Niko and me. He expresses his gratitude as well. Samuel gives his regards, and has told us that he thinks he might find a way to write about your experience in some way. I have taken your advice and purchased that island north of Watertown. Perhaps someday I will be able to visit it, but not yet. Our work is so important, now that we know what is possible. Perhaps someday I will visit you there! One can only imagine. I must return to my work now. Be safe. Love, your great-great-grandfather Hudson Cavalier."

"Okay, that's weird," Tipp said.

"Yeah, I know. Right?" Elina read it one more time just to make sure, but there was simply no making sense of it. She sat, thinking for a moment. Tipp had lost interest and walked over to look at the books in the library.

"You know what I think," Tipp said as he slid books out to look at the covers and then slid them back. "I think that letter and the picture we saw in the sitting room were of our relatives. I think maybe we were just named after somebody else, that's all. Like my middle name is Hudson just like the guy who signed the letter."

"Maybe," Elina said. What her brother was saying made the most sense. She laid the letter flat on the steel mesh floor and slid out her computer tablet. Thumbing over to the right application, she took a picture of the letter and saved it to her files. She looked at the image on her screen. Tapping her pinched fingers onto the screen, she spread them apart to zoom in on the letter. She was studying each word closely when Tipp called out.

"Look at this!" He was holding up a book trying to show her, but it was too far away for her to clearly make out anything except for the fact that it looked really old. She slid her tablet back into its carrying case and stood so as to rejoin her brother on the lower level. By the time she was by his side, Tipp had sat himself down on the floor and was leafing through the book.

"Can I see it?" Elina asked.

"No, I'm looking at it."

"Come on, what is it?"

"It's a book written by none other than Hudson Cavalier," Tipp said.

"Let me see!" Elina pleaded. "Please?"

"You wouldn't let me see the letter," he retorted.

"Well you can look at it now if you'd like," she offered, handing the letter over.

"I don't want to look at it now, I already know what it says. If you'd like, I can read the book to you," Tipp said with a wry grin. He loved throwing things right back at his sister to see how she liked it.

"No, it's fine," Elina said. "I'm going to look around

the rest of the house while you sit here with a book."
With that, Elina walked out of the library leaving Tipp
to himself.

The book was very interesting. Hudson Cavalier was
a scientist, the book said. It seemed to be a journal of the
experiments that he had worked on with someone named
Nikola. They were extremely complex and difficult for Tipp
to completely understand, but he was able to determine
that the experiments had to do with generating electricity.
They were using terms like voltage and electricity and
generator. After just a few moments he could no longer
bear the burden of curiosity. He had to find out what his
sister was doing. He set the book down on the floor and
ran out of the library to find her.

Elina had first gone back to the sitting room, as she
wanted to take a snapshot of the picture they had seen
earlier. Once that was saved in her tablet computer, she
set out to explore more of the house. She stood at the base
of the stairs in the main entryway, thinking about which
area she should investigate first. There was a grumble in
her stomach and the decision was easy: the kitchen.

CHAPTER 5

Alonzo was on his hands and knees, scrubbing the tiled floor when Elina walked in. He stopped and looked up at her, his eyes red and his face flushed. He dragged a sleeve across his face and stood up.

"Can I be of service, Miss Elina?"

"I'm a little hungry, I was just going to fix a sandwich. Can you show me where everything is? I don't want to be a bother," she said to him.

"Nonsense! I will make you the best sandwich your mouth has ever tasted!" He seemed to brighten at the prospect of serving someone. He scooped her up and set her on one of the tall stools that were around the large, butcher block island in the center of the kitchen.

"What would you like? Turkey? Salami? Maybe just peanut butter and jelly?"

"I would love a tomato and ham sandwich, with mayo and salt and pepper, please," she said.

"Ah, you have excellent taste!" he said, spinning towards the large stainless steel refrigerator. He quickly gathered all the ingredients and placed them neatly on the butcher block surface with a bit of a panache. It seemed as if he was putting on a performance, each of his motions seemed grandiose and exaggerated. He spread the mayo with a flourish of his knife, sliced the tomato with lightning speed, held the salt and pepper shaker high in the air, letting the contents snow down upon the sandwich. Finally, with delicate precision, he laid the ham in neat layers onto the bread. After he cut it and placed it gently onto her plate, he brought his fingers to his mouth and made a kiss.

"Bon appetite!"

"Thank you! That was amazing," Elina said.

"You're welcome, miss. I do hope you enjoy it." He set about cleaning up his work area while Elina bit into her afternoon snack. It was just as delicious as she had hoped it would be.

As she finished the sandwich, and as Alonzo finished cleaning up, Elina decided she would interrogate him a bit to see what he knew about the strange letter and picture she had found. She slid her tablet out of its case and set it on the butcher block counter.

"Alonzo, can I ask you a question?" she said.

"Two," he replied.

"What?"

"Well, I guess three now. You have already asked me two questions, so you may proceed with your third," he teased her. Elina just rolled her eyes. It was the type of extreme literalism joke her father loved as well, but made her groan.

"How long did you know Great Grandpa?"

"Ah, I would have to think about that. I knew him for several years before he hired me as his chef. I worked at my family's restaurant in Pensacola, Florida when I first met him. He was an old Navy man, I believe. At least he always wore a naval jacket when he would come down to the base to see how things were going. I never did find out why he came down as much as he did. Anyway, the first time I remember him was the day I received my draft notification. I was eighteen and had been drafted into the Navy to serve in the Vietnam War. I was scared and my mother was just beside herself with grief.

"Now, I have to go back a bit. As much as you enjoyed that sandwich I just made, my specialty is a western omelet. Every time your great-grandfather came in for breakfast, he would order one of my omelets. And every time he would tell me that it was the best omelet he'd ever had. It turns out making a good omelet was pretty important because the day I received my draft notice, your great-grandfather just happened to be walking in. My mother was crying and my father was upset as well, though I never saw him cry. He asked what all the fuss was about, and I handed him the notice. I still remember him reading that notice and shaking his head the whole time. He looked up at me, and you know what he told us? Your great-grandfather told us not to worry. A few days passed and he came in and sat down and, of course, ordered a western omelet. When he got up to leave, he left a letter with his tip. He told me not to open it, but just to go in and hand it to the draft board when I was called.

"I did just what he told me. The morning I was to report to the draft board, I took that letter with me, hoping that it would save me from going to war. I handed it to them, and they opened it and took turns reading it. To my surprise, they released me and told me I was exempted from duty and could go home!"

"What did the letter say?" Elina asked. She had never heard this story before and was absolutely enthralled.

"It said: To whom it may concern, Alonzo Alexandro Jr. serves an important role in the nation's security and is in possession of a specialized skill set that makes him an indispensable entity. Therefore, he is relieved of any active duty responsibilities and shall be exempted from conscription indefinitely. Signed, General William C. Westmorland."

"Okay, I don't get it," Elina said.

"Of course you don't," Alonzo said. "The General was in charge of the entire U.S. military in Vietnam at that time. Somehow your great-grandfather got him to personally sign a paper saying that I didn't have to go to war. Ever! All because your great-grandfather liked my omelets. A week later, he asked me to come work for him up here as his head chef. That was in 1967."

"Wow, that was a long time ago," Elina said.

"When I think about it now, it is. But some days it seems like it just happened. I owe your great-grandfather my life. It breaks my heart that the old guy is gone."

"Yeah, me too," Elina said, patting Alonzo on the arm. "So, since you've lived here for so long, you've probably seen just about everything in this house, right?"

"Actually, no. I was only allowed in the kitchen, sitting room and your great-grandfather's study. In fact, no one, to my knowledge, was ever allowed to wander the house without him."

"Have you ever seen this picture before?" Elina showed him the picture on her tablet that she had taken of the photograph.

"I don't recognize it. The man shares a fair likeness to your great-grandfather when he was younger, but I don't think it's him. He never wore his hair that way. It does look like you and your brother, though. Where did you get this?" Alonzo asked.

"Great Grandpa was looking at it the day he died. He had it in the sitting room," Elina said.

"I'm sorry, I've never seen it before," Alonzo said.

"Maybe I'll ask Sullo. Where is he?"

"The last I knew he was in your great-grandfather's study reviewing documents. He has a lot of paperwork to take care of to settle the estate."

"Okay," Elina said, hopping down from the stool and skipping towards the door. "Thanks for the sandwich, and for the story! It was a good one."

"You're welcome," Alonzo said as Elina left the kitchen. He sighed heavily and looked around the kitchen for a moment. Then, he got back down on the floor and continued scrubbing.

CHAPTER 6

Sullivan O'Grady was reading over the last will and testament of Richard Bartholomew Cavalier, or as the children knew him, Great Grandpa Dickie. Sullo was executor of the will, which meant he was in charge of making sure everything was carried out according to Great Grandpa Dickie's exact wishes. The will had seemed to be a fairly straight forward and basic last will and testament until the last page. Sullo read it again and again.

"Upon the disappearance of Tipp and Elina, you are not to notify the authorities under any circumstances. Rather, you must open the envelope that accompanies this document. Do not open the document until that time," Sullo read aloud.

"What is this craziness, Mr. Cavalier? What form of mischievousness are you up to now?" Sullo asked out loud.

Just then, there was a knock at the door.

"Come in," O'Grady said, setting the paperwork aside.

"It's just me, Sullo," Elina said as she entered the room. "I wanted to ask you about a picture we found."

"Come on in. Where's your brother?"

"Oh, he's still downstairs reading a book." Elina

brought her tablet over to show Sullo the photograph. He studied the photo for a moment.

"Have you ever seen this before?" she asked.

"No. Where did you find it?"

"Great Grandpa Dickie was looking at it the day he died. And then, we found a letter in the library." Elina thumbed over to the next photo to show the image she had taken of the letter. Sullo read it and then handed it back to her.

"The letter was addressed to Tipp and me," Elina said. "What do you think it means?"

"I really don't know. There had been some very peculiar things happening since your great-grandfather's passing," he said.

No sooner had the words left his mouth, when an alarm began to sound. Sullo jumped up from his chair and ran over to a cabinet. Opening the doors, he revealed several flat screen televisions with surveillance video of the estate.

"What is that?" Elina asked, covering her ears.

"It's a security alarm," Sullo said, concentrating on the surveillance video screens. He located the intruder. Someone had just driven a boat up to the dock and was getting out.

"Listen, go find your brother and stay with him until I come and find you," Sullo said. "This is serious."

Elina grabbed her computer tablet and ran out of the

room to get her brother. Sullo raced back to the desk and opened the top drawer. He withdrew a large pistol and checked to make sure it was loaded. He didn't know who the intruder was, but he was going to find out.

Tipp had left the book and began doing some investigating of his own. He heard Elina in the kitchen talking to Alonzo, so he headed down the other wing. The first door he came to was one that the children had never been allowed to enter. He tried the doorknob, but it was locked. The locks were very old fashioned, and would be easy to pick.

He had stored the Houdini lock picking set in the thigh pocket of his cargo pants. In moments, he had the set opened, a torsion wrench and pick selected and inserted into the key hole. It took him just a few seconds to execute his precise maneuvers. With satisfaction, he heard the click of the lock springing open. He tried the knob and this time, it opened. Carefully, Tipp placed the pick and wrench back into the leather wallet and then, slid it into his pocket.

The door revealed a flight of stairs that went down into the cellar. He flicked the switch on the wall and the darkness disappeared under the illumination of the dim bulbs. Tipp thought for a moment that he might go get his sister to go with him, but then, decided against it. A dank, musty smell hit his nose as he descended the steps. The walls were carved out of the bedrock. At first he thought it was a dirt floor, but it too was smoothly-hewn from the bedrock, just covered in a layer of dirt and dust. The steps had led him to a long corridor which now stretched out before him. This was unlike any cellar or basement he had ever seen before. Bulbs hung from the ceiling every ten feet, and Tipp could see doors on each side of the corridor. He slowly walked towards the first door and tried the knob.

Inside, were shelves that went from floor to ceiling. They were stocked with all sorts of canned goods and such. He pressed on to the next, and then the next. Each of the rooms held various supplies. Some were filled with toilet tissue and paper towels. Others had shelves and shelves of light bulbs. It was as if Great Grandpa Dickie had bought everything in bulk so he could remain isolated from the mainland for years, if necessary, yet still be comfortably self-sufficient.

Tipp finally came to the last door just as he heard his sister's voice. He tried the knob and it was unlocked. Unlike the other rooms, this one was not illuminated. He tried on the wall for a switch, but found none.

"Tipp, are you down here?"

"Yeah!"

"What are you doing? There's an emergency!" Elina called to him. She came down several steps.

"What kind of emergency?" he called back to her.

"I don't know. Somebody is at the dock, and Sullo told me to come find you and stay together until Sullo says it's okay."

"Then come here, and bring your tablet. I can't find the light switch," he said to her. He listened as she came down the steps to the corridor. He waved to her, and she waved back.

"Did you find anything cool?"

"No," he replied. "It's nothing but storage. Spaghetti sauce and toilet paper. It's completely stocked. We could live here for years and never leave the island."

"Well, that makes sense. It's not like you can just hop in the car and run to the store from here," Elina said as she arrived by Tipp's side. She took out her tablet and thumbed over to the flashlight application. It filled the screen with white, and she used it to illuminate the room. There were a lot of boxes and machinery, from the looks of it, but to see what was really in the room, they needed to find a light switch.

"There it is," Tipp said. "Shine it back to the left."

Sure enough, on the wall was a large switch that was in the off position. Tipp ran over and grabbed the lever.

"Wait, Tipp. I'm not sure that's the light switch," Elina said. He ignored her and pushed the lever up to the on position. No lights came on, but an electric hum began to fill the room.

"See. It's not a light switch. You just turned something on and we don't even know what. Turn it off," she said. Slowly, however, something did begin to light the room.

"It is a light," Tipp said in defiance. "It just takes a little time to warm up is all. Old lights are like that." He acted like he knew what he was talking about. Elina hated it when he acted like a know-it-all.

As the noise grew louder, so too did the light grow incrementally brighter. They could now make out some of the details of the room. The light was coming from something under a tarp, so Tipp went over and pulled it off, bathing the room in an eerie blue light.

"That's no light like I've ever seen," Elina said. It was a large glowing circle that was attached to a bunch of other machinery in the room by cables. Suddenly there was a crack of electricity as, what looked like, a bolt of lightning shot out from the machine.

"Turn it off!" Elina yelled.

"Yeah, I think that's a good idea," Tipp said. Another bolt of electricity shot out of the machine. "Um, you do it."

"Tipp, shut it off!" Elina yelled.

"Look!" Tipp pointed at the machine. In the center, they could make out, what appeared to be, shadows of two people. Gradually it came into focus, even as electricity began to arc all around them.

"It's some kind of old television," Elina said. "Shut it off before it catches something on fire."

One of the men was reaching towards them, when there was an unexpected burst of electricity. They couldn't believe their eyes. A hand was reaching right out of the machine towards them!

"Cool, it's a hologram!" Tipp's eyes widened as he reached for the three-dimensional hand.

"No, Tipp. I don't think that's what it is," Elina said, with skepticism and caution in her voice. She grabbed his arm as he reached out. Suddenly the man's hand grabbed Tipp's arm and pulled him. Tipp let out a yelp of surprise, and Elina grabbed tighter to try to hold him.

"He's got me!" Tipp screeched.

A great burst of energy occurred, and the room went dark.

"Who are you and what do you want?" Sullo had the pistol in hand, but he wasn't pointing it at the stranger from the boat. Not yet, at least.

"At ease, Sullivan," the man said as he walked up the dock towards him. "I'm a friend."

Sullivan hadn't recognized him over the video feed, so he was willing to give him the benefit of the doubt.

"Who are you?"

"Jeremiah Conklin, FBI and close friend of Peter Cavalier's," the man said as he came up to Sullo. He was not quite six feet tall, but looked to be very fit and very strong. He had dark skin, dark hair, and was wearing beige khakis and a blue shirt.

"Mind if I see some identification?"

"Not at all," Conklin said, retrieving his wallet from his back pocket and opening up his badge. Sullivan took it and looked it over. Satisfied, he handed it back.

"What can I do for you," Sullivan said as he slid his pistol into the rear waistband of his pants.

"I've come to make sure the children are safe. Something has happened. I'm sure you know that Peter and Asta went to Australia to look for Peter's parents," Conklin said.

"Yes. I knew about that."

"Well, they've gone missing as well. They were working with our agents there in Australia when they disappeared from their hotel room. Something is going on, and I came to make sure that the children were safe. Peter and I, we go back a long time."

"Okay," Sullivan said. "Let's go up to the house. Let's try not to scare the children. They just lost their great-grandfather two days ago."

"What happened," Conklin asked as they walked.

"Old age. The man was ninety-one."

"Wow. I hope I live to be that old," Conklin said.

"Me too. He was healthy right up until he passed away. Nicest guy you'd ever meet, too," Sullo said, opening the front door to the house.

Alonzo came rushing up the cellar stairs and out into the entry way with a frantic look on his face.

"Alonzo, what is it?" Sullivan asked.

"The children," he said out of breath. "They've disappeared!"

CHAPTER 7

There was a flash of bright light and then darkness. Blinding darkness. They were laying on the floor, still holding hands, but they weren't in the cellar of their great-grandfather's island mansion anymore. Both of them lay motionless, as it hurt to move. It felt like the tingling sensation of when a foot or hand falls asleep, except it was all over their bodies, from their toes to their eyelids. After a few moments, the discomfort began to subside, and they could move.

Brother and sister sat up to take in their surroundings.

"Impossible," someone said. There was smoke and it was dark, so they couldn't make out to whom the words belonged.

"Are you okay?" Elina asked her brother. Even her lungs tingled, and it made her cough a little.

"I think so," Tipp responded. "What happened?"

"I don't know. The last thing I remember was your arm getting grabbed and then poof, we were here," she said.

"Yeah, me too."

"Remarkable," the voice said again.

"Who said that?" Elina said, grabbing her brother's hand more for her own reassurance than for his.

"Allow me to introduce myself," the voice said in the darkness. The smell of sulfur filled the air as a match was lit. They watched as the single orange flame was carried across the room, shielded by a hand, and held to a lamp. A small key was turned on the side of the lamp and gas was allowed in. A larger flame grew within the lamp glass and threw illumination throughout the room. It was then that the children could see who it was that had spoken. "I'm Hudson, and this is Nikola."

"Very pleased to meet the two of you," Nikola said. He was pulling himself off the floor and rubbing his arm in the process. He uprighted an overturned stool and perched his tall, gangly frame upon it. He had dark hair and sunken eyes. A dark mustache obscured his upper lip, and his clothing looked like something out of a Sherlock Holmes movie.

"Perhaps, you could explain from where it is the two of you have come," Nikola said.

"First, tell us where we are," Elina said. She watched as the man who had called himself Hudson went round the room, lighting lamps on the walls with the long thin match. Her eyes adjusted to the dim light. After having just experienced the sudden, brilliant flash, it took a moment. She could see that they were sitting on the floor of some sort of workshop. It was filled with work benches, upon which were tools and scraps of metal and wood. Behind her was a great machine that was identical to the one Tipp had found in the cellar, except for some of the cables and wires that had been attached to the one they had discovered.

"You are in the laboratory of Nikola Tesla, and I am his assistant," Hudson said.

"But, where are we?" Tipp asked.

"Why, you're in New York City, Manhattan to be precise, Grand Avenue to be even more precise," Hudson said. "Now, answer me, from where did you two children appear as if out of nowhere?"

"We were in the cellar of our great-grandfather's house, standing in front of a big machine just like this one, when an arm reached out and grabbed Tipp and pulled us here," Elina said.

"And where was this house of your great-grandfather's?" Tesla asked.

"On an island," Tipp said.

"An island!" Tesla echoed.

"On the St. Lawrence River. You know, the Thousand Islands," Elina added.

"The St. Lawrence River, indeed," Tesla copied again. His voice took on a high pitched tone, as he said it.

"Why do you keep repeating us?" Elina asked.

"Because, I am of the belief that you have just experienced an event of such enormous proportions that all of humanity will look back on this and realize that the history of mankind forever changed from this moment onward!" Tesla said with a level of pride in his voice.

"This machine has proven that not only can energy be transferred wirelessly through the ether, but that matter, flesh and blood, can be transferred through time and space."

"Whoa, what? Transferred through time?" Tipp asked. "What year is this?"

"What do you mean?" Hudson asked, completing his circuit of the room, lighting all the lamps. "Why, it's 1891, of course. May 25th, 1891." As Hudson drew near to them again, a wave of recognition swept over Elina.

"It's you!" she exclaimed. "Tipp, it's him!"

"Who?" Tipp asked.

"Yes, who exactly do you believe me to be?" Hudson asked.

Without another word, Elina grabbed at the carrying case which was still strapped over her shoulder. She slid out the tablet computer, hoping that it hadn't been hurt by the electrical shock she'd just experienced. To her relief, it started up, and she thumbed over to the picture.

"Look," she said, showing it first to Tipp, and then to the men.

"No way," Tipp said. "That's creepy."

"Incredible," Hudson said.

"Marvelous," Nikola said. Neither of them were talking about the identical resemblance of the man in the photo to Hudson himself. Rather, both were enthralled with the piece of technology that they held in their hands.

"Do you know what's going on here?" Tipp asked his sister.

"I think so," she replied.

"Did we just travel through time to 1891?" Tipp asked.

"I think so," she answered again.

"Whoa."

"Yeah," Elina said. "Whoa." The children stood and began to look around the room. Tipp went to the window to look around outside, and saw horse drawn carriages on the cobblestone streets below. Gaslight street lamps flickered in the darkness, and people strolled down the sidewalks in clothing that looked like they were straight out of an old movie.

"Okay, this is too cool," Tipp said. His sister wasn't so sure about how cool the situation was.

"I think this is just a dream. I think we just got shocked by the machine, and this is all just a very elaborate dream," she said. She was starting to breathe a little heavy, like she did before she started to cry.

Tipp pinched her arm hard.

"Ow! What did you do that for?"

"I guess you're not dreaming," he said with a gleeful grin. "This really happened! We traveled through time. That is our great-great-grandfather Hudson Cavalier. Elina, we are totally time-travelers!"

"I need to sit down," Elina said, looking for a chair. She spotted one across the room and numbly walked towards it to sit. She needed to calm herself down and stop hyperventilating. She had a tendency to get overly excited and breathe too deeply, too quickly, and then pass out. It had happened several times in her life already. She practiced the breathing tips her father had taught her; slowly, in through the nose, hold it for a moment, then out through the mouth.

Without warning, there was a loud noise, like someone ripping through burlap.

"Tipp!"

"Sorry," he said. "I had too!" He started giggling, and this got Elina giggling as well.

"If I smell it, you're in trouble," she said.

"If you smell it, you're in trouble," he said back to her, laughing. "Who knew time traveling gives you the toots?"

For whatever reason, having her brother pass gas and laugh about it made her feel better. Under normal circumstances, she would have been yelling for her mother or father to scold him, but right now they were not under, what one would call, normal circumstances. It felt good to have some sense of normalcy in what had become a very upside down few days.

"Tipp, what are we going to do?"

"What do you mean?"

"How are we going to get home?" she asked.

"We just turn the machine back on and go home," he said, oversimplifying the matter as usual.

"Uh, well, it may not be so simplistic," Hudson chimed in. He had torn his attention away from the computer tablet for a moment and overheard the conversation. "It would appear that, just on brief inspection, several of the machine's components have burned. It will take some time to replace them."

"How long will that take?" Elina asked.

"Days. Weeks," Nikola quipped, still fascinated with Elina's device.

"Or perhaps longer," Hudson said more practically. "At this point, we are not even sure what is in need of repair or if it is even possible to repair. We may need to completely rebuild."

"Well, if things burned out with this machine," Tipp said. "It's possible that the machine back in the cellar could have burned out as well."

"Quite possible," Hudson replied.

"So this machine AND that machine would have to be repaired to get us back," Tipp theorized.

"An entirely plausible conclusion," said Hudson.

"So, we could be stuck here permanently," Elina cried. "What are we going to do?"

Finally, Tesla stood and handed Elina her tablet. Without saying another word, he walked over to his machine and began a cursory inspection. As he looked over the parts that needed to be repaired, he spoke to himself in a low voice, as if creating a grocery list of the items he would need to acquire or build to make it work again. Everyone in the room watched him as he went about this task. He stood at last, and rubbed his fingers on his chin for a moment.

"Seventeen days," he said. "Seventeen days of working tirelessly without letup to repair this machine. I must fabricate twenty-six different components to complete the machine. If I only sleep four hours each day, I may be able to shave off two additional days."

"But, what about the other machine, the one back in our time?" Elina asked.

"Let me think on that a bit more," Nikola said. "A solution will present itself." He spoke with a grandiosity that gave the children a sense of security. He sounded like he had everything well under control, and that's exactly what they needed at that moment.

"If you ready a list of the items you need, I can set about retrieving them in the morn," Hudson said. "For now, I think it best that we get these children to some suitable sleeping quarters. It's not good for a child to be up past nine o'clock."

"My dear Hudson, agreed! Pragmatic as always. I shall ready a list for you and send you out in the morning as you suggest."

"Children, if you will follow me, I can put you up in my quarters. They are but a few blocks walk. I have pillows and blankets that will suit you just fine."

"What do you think?" Elina asked Tipp.

"What other choice do we have?"

"I know," she agreed. "Okay, we'll go with you."

With that, they bid farewell to Nikola and followed Hudson down the stairs to street level. It was quite dark, and the sky was gray, threatening rain. They spoke quietly as they walked.

"I must say, I'm not entirely convinced that you children are from the future, though that device you have is quite amazing. I was tempted to label it a simple trick, but it is far too advanced. It's clearly of a superior technological civilization. So tell me, from what year have you traveled?"

"2013," the children said at the same time.

"One hundred twenty-two years in the future. Amazing! The questions that fill my mind about what life must be like then! Surely, all disease has been eradicated. How long can people live?"

"Well, Great Grandpa Dickie was ninety-one. He just died two days ago. Er, two days ago for us," Elina said.

"Ninety-one doesn't seem that old at all, considering we have people now that live that long. Of course, we have many more that succumb to all sorts of diseases at a much younger age. What other fantastic things have been discovered in your time? Have you traveled to the other planets? Have you traveled to Mars?"

"No, but men have landed on the moon!" Tipp had read about the Apollo moon landings the previous summer. There wasn't a piece of information he hadn't devoured on the subject. Of course, after three straight months of dropping interesting facts about the landings on the rest of his family, his father decided to find another subject for him to digest. That's when he got hooked on baseball.

"The moon! How amazing! Have you two been to the moon?" Hudson asked.

"No," Tipp said with a laugh. "Only twelve men landed on the moon. The manned moon landings spanned a 41 month time period from July 12th, 1969 through December 14th, 1972. People haven't gone back since then."

"Why did they stop?"

"Well, there are a lot of theories on that. I think it's because they didn't find anything up there. I mean the moon is cool and everything, it helps with the tides and all, but it turns out it's just a big rock with lots of dirt on it," Tipp said. "After that, they started sending rockets and satellites out to other planets. They landed a rover on Mars and sent back a ton of pictures. That was pretty cool. But, there's nothing on Mars either. At least there hasn't been any life discovered yet. They might find some bacteria or something, who knows."

"Interesting. And how is it that a boy of your age can know so much about this?" Hudson inquired.

"It's all on the internet," Elina said. "You just type in a keyword and you can find all the information you need."

"The internet, explain that to me."

"It's like where you go to get information and play games and stuff," Elina said.

"You know, the computer tablet that you guys were so amazed by?" Tipp asked.

"Is that what the device is called? A computer tablet?" Hudson asked back.

"Yes. Anyway, that's just one kind of computer. In 2013, there are millions and millions of computers all over the world. The internet is how they are all connected. You don't store all the information on your own computer, you go out to other people's computers. Like for baseball scores or -"

"They have baseball in 2013?"

"Sure! We go to see the Mets play all the time. You like baseball too?" Tipp asked.

"Absolutely. We have two teams, the Brooklyn Grooms and the New York Giants. Though, last year the Giants lost many players to the new league. The league folded, as most of us suspected it would. The Giants are looking good once again. The Grooms, on the other hand, won the league last year!"

"If we're going to be here for seventeen days, maybe we could go see a game?" Tipp asked excitedly.

"Perhaps we could," Hudson replied. "Here we are, my home for the time being."

It was a rather drab looking four-story building. The entry way was seven steps up from the street and through a narrow door. They took the stairs to the top floor and went down a corridor to the very back of the building.

Hudson used his key to open the door. It was pitch black inside, and he moved about to light a lamp. When the light finally shone on the room, Tipp and Elina were not impressed. It was a small, twelve foot by twelve foot room with a bed, a small couch, a chair and a dresser with a bowl and pitcher on it.

"This is it?" Elina asked.

"Well I know it's not the Taj Mahal, but it's not bad for a newly married man of meager wages," Hudson said defensively. "But, I have some patents pending. Once the patents are officially registered and can be sold for commercial use, I will start earning better wages. Besides, I'm in the laboratory most of the time. Also, and more importantly, I might add, I should not have to explain my living arrangements to children. You're fortunate I'm not making you sleep on the street tonight."

"Where are we going to sleep?" Tipp asked. "There's only one bed?"

"Well I assumed you two could share the bed and I could sleep on the couch. Truthfully, I think I will be spending most nights back at the laboratory with Nikola, as is my custom. Make yourselves comfortable. The water closet is down the hall," he said.

"What's a water closet?" Tipp asked.

"It's uh, where you go to, you know," Hudson stumbled over his words.

"It's what they call bathrooms here," Elina said matter-of-factly. "I read it in a book called *The Great Brain*."

"We don't get our own bathroom?" Tipp grumbled.

"I'm sure everyone gets their own everything in the future, but here, we share. So, you two will be sharing a bed, and in the event of needing to relieve yourselves, you will share the water closet," Hudson said with a level of sternness in his voice. "And that will be the end of it, understood?"

"Yes," the children chorused. They climbed into the bed, with their clothes still on, and within moments they both drifted off to sleep.

Hudson stayed awake for a bit longer, a question running through his head. How was it that the children had come to appear as they had? They had mentioned a similar machine. Perhaps, he thought, the machines opened a pathway, a connection across time, which allowed the children to make their journey. There was so much he didn't understand about it all. Undoubtedly, Tesla had already worked out the answers. They would surely discuss them in the morning. With that, he drifted off to sleep.

CHAPTER 8

The children awoke to sunlight streaming through the lone window in the small room. Hudson was nowhere to be seen, though a blanket and pillow were still on the couch. There wasn't a clock in the room, so the children had no idea what time it was. Elina just knew she had to use the bathroom. She hopped out of bed and walked down the hallway to the door marked W.C.

It smelled bad, but appeared clean, and she was able to relieve herself quickly. She pulled on the chain to flush the toilet, and was impressed that it pretty much worked the same as the toilets in 2013. She washed her hands and dried them on a towel. She heard the floors creaking outside and thought she also heard one of the doors open to another room, so she ran back to their room and shut the door. Tipp had rolled over and gone back to sleep, obviously forgetting where and when they were. So, Elina went over to the window to see what she could of the place they were in.

She wasn't rewarded with much of a view. The window looked out into the alleyway behind the building, and people had strung up their laundry in the morning sun. Sheets, shirts, underwear and socks all decorated dozens of clotheslines in the alley. She couldn't see past them down to street level, so numerous and being blown by the wind as they were.

After a few minutes, Tipp finally decided it was time to get up. He went down the hall to the water closet and returned after just a short time.

"So what are we supposed to do?" Tipp asked.

"I don't know. Wait here until Hudson comes back to get us, I guess," Elina replied.

"That doesn't sound like much fun," Tipp said.

"I know."

They watched out the window for a time, looking up at the sky as the clouds drifted by. With an effort, they were able to get the window open a crack so they could hear the sounds of the city echoing down the alleyway.

"It's weird," Tipp said. "I don't feel like we're in a different time. I mean, I feel like my normal self, just in another place. It's like, I feel like we're visiting someplace else, you know? Like when we take the yacht on a cruise or fly someplace."

"The only difference is, we can't hop on a plane and go home," Elina said. "I don't know if we'll ever be able to go home."

"What did you just say?" Tipp asked suddenly.

"I said, I don't know if we'll ever be able to go home."

"On the front of our apartment building in Brooklyn, do you remember the date?" Tipp asked, hopping up from the couch where he had been lounging.

"1873."

"So if this is 1891, then our building exists, it's already been built. We could go see our house!" Tipp was heading towards the door.

"We can't."

"Why not," he countered.

"Because we have to wait here for Hudson to come back," Elina reasoned.

"Who knows when that will be?" Tipp said. "We can write him a note." Tipp went over to the dresser where he had seen some letter writing supplies. He retrieved a piece of paper and got out the pen. He had actually used an ink dipping pen before in his art class, so he wasn't at all confused when he saw the ink jar and pen with metal nib.

"We can't go out like in public dressed like this. Our clothes, they don't fit in," Elina argued. She was as eager and curious to see their house in Brooklyn as Tipp, but if they went out dressed as they were, they would raise surely raise suspicion. After seeing all of the time travel movies they had seen, Elina knew that was a bad thing. You were supposed to blend in so no one knew you were a time traveler.

Tipp was wearing a t-shirt with a comic book hero screen printed on the front and a long-sleeved insulated top underneath. His pants were khakis with cargo pockets, very baggy. He had on his favorite pair of Converse brand sneakers with bright green laces.

Elina wore a pink t-shirt with a white long-sleeved

shirt under it. Her cargo pants were also khaki, and, of course, her pull on leather boots with fleece lining. They would stand out just a bit.

"Look out the window," Tipp said with a grin. "I'm sure we can find what we need out there." He was pointing down at the lines and all the clothes they held. There might be something there they could use.

"We can't steal somebody else's clothes," Elina scolded.

"We're not stealing, we're borrowing. We'll give them back," Tipp reasoned.

"I don't know," Elina was starting to cave in to his scheme.

"Come on, we'll be back before they even notice the clothes are gone," Tipp said.

"Okay," Elina conceded. She did want to see their house.

"Alright," Tipp said. "I'll write the letter, since I know how to use this type of pen, and you go get the clothes."

"I know how to use those pens too! You go get the clothes."

"Listen, whatever dress I bring back, you will hate. But me? I don't care what I wear. So, whatever you pick out is fine," Tipp said. Elina had to admit, he had a point.

They forced open the window even further and Elina climbed out onto the steel fire escape. She could reach quite a few of the lines by descending the ladder and reaching out.

"Plus, you're not afraid of heights," Tipp said to himself with a gulp and went back into the room to write the letter.

It read simply: "Dear Hudson, We went to Brooklyn to see our house. Be back soon. Tipp and Elina."

In just a few moments, Elina had returned with two boys shirts and jackets.

"You can wear your pants with the shirt and jacket," Elina said. "I think it will look fine."

"What are you going to wear?" Tipp asked.

"There weren't any dresses," Elina said, throwing the clothes on the floor and flopping onto the bed. "I don't want to go."

"Come on," Tipp said. "You can just pretend. Like acting. Remember, when there weren't enough boys in your class to play all the male roles when you guys did that play and one of the girls had to be George Washington? All the girls wanted to be George Washington."

"That's because he got to ride the big white horse," Elina said.

"Listen, just try it on," Tipp said. "You don't want to wear a stinkin' dress anyway, right?"

"But I wanted to wear one of the dresses like the ladies wear. Everybody will think I'm a boy!" Elina said as she reluctantly pulled on the larger of the two shirts.

Tipp's shirt and jacket fit perfectly. Elina was right, the khaki pants didn't look too terribly out of place with the shirt and jacket. He dug into Hudson's dresser and found a hat. He stood in front of the mirror. He suddenly realized that the hat was the same as was in the picture he'd seen in the photo, though the shirt and jacket were different.

Elina's shirt and jacket were too big, but she rolled up the sleeves and tucked in the shirt. She too found a hat and tucked her hair up into it. She had been right, she did look like a boy.

All dressed in their borrowed clothing, Elina and Tipp prepared to leave. Tipp was happy he didn't have to leave behind his Houdini kit. It was tucked safely into the leg pocket of his cargo pants. It was always good to be prepared.

Elina's over-the-shoulder bag fit right in with the rest of her outfit so she took her computer tablet with them. She looked like a messenger boy. With everything in order, they tried the lock on the door to make sure they could open it again once they returned.

They went down the four flights of stairs and into the lobby. Neither of them remembered anyone being at the front desk the previous night, but there was a man in a crimson and gold uniform standing behind the desk now. He eyed them keenly as they came down the final flight of stairs.

"What are you two up to, then?" he asked them as they walked passed his post.

"Nothing," Elina said. "Just going for a walk."

"No, I mean, what was you two doin' upstairs in the first place?" A portion of the counter was hinged, and he lifted it to get after them. Tipp took off in a run out the front door, with Elina behind him. They navigated the steps and were a block away before they stopped to catch their breath. He hadn't bothered to chase them after they had left the lobby, so they had escaped.

"How are we going to get back in now?" Elina asked her brother.

"We'll find a way. Come on. Let's get over to the Brooklyn Bridge," he said, pulling her by the hand. They headed east and found themselves on Broadway after just two blocks. Nothing looked familiar, but both of them knew that if you went as far south as you could on Broadway, one only had to take a left through the park to find the Brooklyn Bridge.

As they walked, they saw that the street was torn up and men were laying down tracks in the center. Hundreds of men were working, bringing in the rails, aligning them, and then driving in spikes to keep the rails in place. They were so enthralled by the construction, that they nearly collided with a woman riding a bicycle. An elderly gentleman kindly whisked them out of the way at the last moment.

"Ridiculous!" he called after her. "The very idea of a woman riding a bicycle! Next, they will want to vote or be President!" He tugged at his white beard with disgust. Tipping his hat to the children, he wished them good day.

He continued walking along the sidewalk, clicking his cane against the stones as he went.

"We need to be careful," Elina told her brother. "We're not used to this place. Keep your eyes open and be prepared, like Dad always says."

"Go together, stay together, come back together. The buddy system saves lives," Tipp imitated his father's deeper voice. They both laughed for a moment, but deep down inside they also wished he was here with them now. He would be so fascinated by the architecture of the buildings all around, and especially of construction techniques the men were using to lay the tracks in the street.

Looking north, up Manhattan Island, the children didn't recognize anything they saw. No Empire State Building, no Chrysler Building, none of the skyscrapers that they grew up seeing almost every day were there. Most of them wouldn't be built for another fifty or more years.

The people were certainly different as well. All of the men wore hats, and none of the women wore pants, they were all in dresses! Elina wished she had a dress like some of the ones she saw the ladies wearing. She didn't want to be forced to wear one, she wanted to be able to have the choice to wear one if she wanted, was all. She used to have elaborate tea parties where her mother and her would have some of the girls over and they would dress up in amazing gowns with white gloves up to the elbows and huge hats and button up shoes and they would sip tea and eat little shortbread cookies. Even though she was all grown up and now ten, Elina wished she could still do that baby stuff sometimes. Seeing all the ladies dressed in the beautiful gowns and with the beautiful hats, made her feel like playing dress up again.

There were mustaches and beards on just about every man that walked by, and many of them carried canes, whether it appeared as if they needed them or not.

"Look how thin everyone is," Elina commented. "I guess if you have to walk everywhere, you don't get fat."

"No drive-thrus either," Tipp agreed. A man walked past them and tossed a newspaper into an overflowing trash cart. Tipp reached over and grabbed it. He was busy looking over the front page when he was suddenly grabbed by the collar and whacked across the back of the head.

"And just what do you think you're doin,' young lad?" said a booming voice behind him. Tipp tried to twist out of the grip, but was held so far up in the air that the tips of his toes barely touched the stone sidewalk.

"Ow!" He yelled. "Let go!"

"I'll let go a ya when ya answer my question!" the voice said.

"I was just grabbing the newspaper," Tipp answered.

"Ah, jus grabbin' tha newspaper. Did ya pay for tha newspaper ya was jus grabbin'?"

"No, it was in the garbage can," Tipp said, still struggling to free himself. He had finally twisted around to see who was holding him, and it was a tall policeman, in a navy colored uniform. The man had a huge round face and a large red mustache.

"Ah, so it mus be your garbage can then, no?"

"No," Tipp answered.

"Then it do not belong to ya! Give it here and get outta my sight before I put ya over my knee. Got it?" the policeman bellowed and it made Tipp shiver. He'd always been taught that policemen were friends and could be trusted, but this one certainly seemed less than friendly. Tipp found himself getting thrown to the ground, where he scraped his hands and knees. It made him mad. He turned around and stood up clenching his jaw with his fists at his side.

"Oh, a scrapper! If it's a fight ya want, I can arrange it, laddie!" The policeman started after him, but Elina grabbed Tipp by the hand and forced him to follow her down the sidewalk. They ran as fast as their feet could carry them. The bully cop gave chase for a bit, but lost interest. They could hear him barking at them to stay off his beat if they knew what was good for them.

"That was crazy," Tipp said. "I just wanted to read the newspaper."

"I know. I don't know what his problem was," Elina said. They had paid little attention to the theaters they were passing. They held names of productions like "A Trip to Chinatown" or "Pillars of Society." They didn't seem interesting at all. Not like the ones their mother and father had taken them to, like *Phantom of the Opera*, *The Lion King* or *Mary Poppins*.

They continued down Broadway past bakeries and

clothing stores. A grocer had fruits and vegetables laid out in bins, and chalk drawn signs advertised prices like a penny a pound for Bartlett pears or two pounds of Empire apples for one cent. Neither of the children had any money in their pockets, and even if they did, it wouldn't have been worth anything in 1891. As they walked past the food, they both suddenly realized how hungry they were.

"We didn't eat breakfast, what are we going to do?" Tipp asked his sister. Unlike her, he hadn't had a delicious sandwich from Alonzo the night before. "I'm starving."

"Me, too. We could walk back and try to find Hudson's lab," Elina offered. She hadn't even thought about how they would eat for the next couple of weeks. She had just assumed that they would be provided for, as they always had been. Here, however, they were more or less on their own. At ages eight and ten respectively, Tipp and Elina were frightened by the realization. After a few moments, however it didn't seem as scary. After all, they were very smart children.

"I have an idea," Tipp said.

"What?"

He explained his plan to his sister, and she liked it very much.

CHAPTER 9

"Come see the Amazing Cavalier perform his magic trick. Watch him make a picture come to life before your very eyes! Just one penny!" Elina was announcing to the people who passed by on the sidewalk. Most people paid no heed, but then a gentleman with a grayish-white hair and a broad gray mustache stopped.

"What are you prattling on about, young sir?" he asked in a friendly way.

"My brother, the Amazing Cavalier, will perform a magic trick for just one penny. He will make a picture come to life right in the frame!"

"Well, now. It must be quite the magic trick for you to charge a whole penny! I tell you what, show me the magic trick and then I'll decide if it was worth a penny," the man said with a crooked smile. He took out a pipe, knocked it on the heel of his boot, and then stuffed it full of tobacco from a small pouch. He struck a match and began to puff away.

Elina went over to Tipp to confer with him about the offer. They went back and forth for a moment and finally Elina returned.

"The Amazing Cavalier has accepted your offer,

though he promises that the trick is worth far more than just a penny," Elina said. She took the man by the hand and walked him over to Tipp, who was hiding Elina's computer tablet behind his back.

A still image of a ballet dancer was on the screen. Tipp waved his hand over the screen.

"Hocus, pocus, out of focus, take a chance and start to dance!" Tipp exclaimed as he touched the screen with his finger. The ballet dancer leapt across the screen in her pink and white costume, followed by a male performer who chased after her, then lifted her by the waist and tossed her several feet in the air. She landed gracefully. Tipp tapped the screen again and it paused.

The man's pipe had fallen from his mouth and landed on the stone sidewalk, spilling out the smoldering tobacco. In a moment, he composed himself and bent to pick up his pipe.

"Son, I have seen some amazing things in my time, but if that doesn't just beat all!" He exclaimed. "I will say, that was certainly worth a penny, and one for you sir, for being such a good barker! If I might inquire, how is it that you managed such an amazing trick?"

"Oh, a magician never tells his secrets," Tipp said, placing the computer tablet behind his back.

"Quite right, quite right. And what is your name, young sir?"

"The Amazing Cavalier," Tipp replied with a smile.

"Well certainly your first name isn't 'Amazing', now is it?"

"My name is Tipp, and this is my, er brother El," he said.

"What peculiar and interesting names, Tipp and El Cavalier," the man said. He fished into his pocket and produced two pennies and handed one each to the children. "I go by the name of Twain. Mark Twain. I've been known to write a thing or two in my time. And I must say, I should like to write about the likes of you two someday."

"You're THE Mark Twain?" Elina asked, skeptically. "You wrote 'Tom Sawyer' and 'Huckleberry Finn'?"

"Indeed I am, and indeed I have. I'm so very pleased that you've heard of the three of us," Mark Twain said.

"Heard of you? You're famous and your books are classics! Everybody has to read them," Tipp said. He had only read an abridged version of Tom Sawyer. It had pictures on every other page, and he had only been six when he read it, but it still counted in his mind.

"Oh, dear, dear, Amazing Tipp Cavalier, if everyone HAD to read them, why, I'd be a very rich man! Alas, I am not," he said. "Perhaps some day."

He pulled a watch from his vest pocket to check the time, and then slid it back.

"I must be going now. I've a meeting with a man who is working on a machine that will revolutionize printing," Twain said with sweeping arms and a smile that pushed his mustache up at an odd angle. "I hope to meet you again someday, Amazing Tipp Cavalier and brother, El. Good day to you both!"

With that, Mark Twain walked on up Broadway, away from the children, whistling a tune and shaking his head.

"That was awesome!" Tipp said.

"I can't wait to tell Mom and Dad that we met the real life Mark Twain!" Elina said. No sooner had the words left her lips, when she realized that she may never get the opportunity to tell them. "I miss them. I want to go home."

"Me too," Tipp said. "But, I'm hungry. Let's go buy some food."

With their two cents combined, they were able to buy two apples, a piece of cheese and a small bread roll. They broke the cheese and roll into two equal parts, or as equal as they could make them, and they gobbled down the morsels. There was almost nothing left of the apple cores when they were through, but they dutifully tossed them into the garbage cart that was parked near the street.

Both were still hungry, but they were no longer starving. They made their way down Broadway, through the small park and over to the Brooklyn Bridge. Horses with carriages crowded the bridge, even as people walked across. Trolleys full of people rode on steel rails and were pulled by teams of horses. Elina and Tipp had spent all of their money on the tiny portion of food, otherwise they would have loved to have hopped on the trolley for a ride.

The bridge made them feel just a little bit like they were home. Just across the river, where they were used to seeing the giant letters spelling out "Watchtower" perched atop the tan factory buildings at the end of the bridge, were just wooden warehouses, and docks for the ships. There was no Manhattan Bridge, none of the buildings that looked familiar at all. They hoped that their own building would be standing where they remembered it to be. As they walked under the Brooklyn Bridge towers they looked up, and for a brief moment, they were in the New York they knew. The bridge transcended time that way.

Smoke was billowing out of stacks all across the city. It was something you couldn't really see when you were walking the streets, but from a distance, black smoke could clearly be seen rising into the air. Most people were heating with coal or wood. When the wind shifted, you could always smell a bit of smoke in the air.

Slowly, they made their way across the Brooklyn Bridge, watching all of the boats go by on the East River. Out in New York Harbor, they saw a familiar site. The Statue of Liberty, with her arm raising the torch, standing as proud as they had always remembered her. They stopped half way across the bridge to reflect for a moment.

"Isn't it amazing that this bridge, the Statue of Liberty, and so much of the rest of it is still around in our day?" Elina asked, more to herself than to her brother.

"Yeah. It's kind of weird. Like something out of a movie," Tipp replied. He also found it fascinating that all the people living their lives all around them would all be dead before he or his sister were ever born. It was almost too overwhelming a thought for his eight-year-old mind to comprehend.

"It's too bad we didn't go back to when Great Grandpa Dickie was a kid. That would have been fun," Tipp said.

"He was born in 1922, so maybe like 1930 or 1932? That would have been awesome!" Elina agreed. They leaned on the railing and watched the boats for a bit more before they continued on across the bridge.

It didn't take long for them to find their apartment building. It looked fresh and new, and it was very strange to not be able to run inside and up to their apartment on the third and fourth floors. They stood on the sidewalk outside the building for several minutes, gazing up at it.

"Do you want to go inside?" Tipp asked.

"I don't know, do you?"

"I don't know," he echoed. "Part of me does and part of me doesn't. I'm worried we'll never see it like it is now, er, when we live there, here, I mean."

"I know, I feel the same way," Elina said. "Well, if we're here for weeks and weeks, maybe we can come back and go inside. For now, we should go back and try to find Hudson and Nikola's lab."

"Okay," Tipp said.

They walked across the street and started heading back towards the bridge, but stopped. Two kids who looked to be about their ages were coming down the steps from their building. They were holding their parents' hands. The mother and father were smiling and laughing while the children were skipping along the sidewalk.

Elina and Tipp watched the family walk to the end of the street. The scene reminded them both of their own family. Of a typical day in their life on a normal weekend going to catch a train to a ballgame or the museum.

"I really want to go home," Tipp said.

"Me too," Elina replied. "If you had just left that switch alone we wouldn't be in this mess."

"It's not my fault!" Tipp replied.

"It is, too!"

"Is not," Tipp pushed his sister. She tried to push him back, but he moved out of the way. She tried to get him again, but he was too quick. He ran down the sidewalk and she chased after him. He laughed and mocked her.

"Elina, big behinda!" he called after her.

"Be quiet! Tipp!"

Just then, a carriage careened around the corner and came up onto the curb. Tipp stopped short, but the carriage was heading right for him. Elina crashed into him and pushed him out of the way at the last moment.

They tumbled into a pile on the sidewalk, the carriage wheels rolling on the sidewalk, narrowly missing them both.

"Watch where you're going, then!" the driver of the carriage yelled at them as he rode off, down the street.

"Whoa," Tipp said, catching his breath. "You saved my life."

"Don't call me that again," Elina said.

"Okay. I won't," Tipp agreed.

They got to their feet, brushed themselves off, and headed back towards the Brooklyn Bridge.

CHAPTER 10

They took a moment at the center of the bridge to gaze at Lady Liberty again before they headed back into Manhattan. It didn't take them long before they were back in front of Hudson's apartment building.

"So, what are we going to do?" Elina asked.

"About what?"

"The doorman," she replied.

"Oh," Tipp knitted his brow. He'd forgotten all about the short chase they'd had that morning. Getting past the doorman was going to be a bit of a challenge. Of course, they could just make a run for it and try to outrace him up the stairs.

"Hmmm," Elina was trying to come up with a plan when suddenly she was shoved from behind.

"What's the idea, then?" A boy said from behind her.

"Excuse me?" Elina said with a huff.

"Excuse you!" the boy said.

"Hey, don't touch my sister!" Tipp said. He balled up his fists, ready for a tussle.

"Those are our clothes," the boy said.

"What?" Elina stammered.

"You heard us," a smaller boy, almost exactly Tipp's size, said. "Those are our clothes. You stole them off our mother's clothesline this morning. This is our building."

Tipp and Elina shared a glance with each other, and then broke into a run. They ran down the sidewalk, dodging pedestrians as they went. The two other boys gave chase, the leather soles of their shoes slapping against the sidewalk loudly.

Tipp and Elina rounded the corner and practically ran into the bully policeman that had almost boxed Tipp's ears earlier in the day. Elina grabbed Tipp by the arm and they crossed the busy street. The boys were still hot on their heels.

Elina ducked down an alley in an attempt to lose their pursuers, but it was a bad move. The alley was a dead end, and the boys had seen the move.

Tipp and Elina were trapped.

"Listen," Elina said, gasping for air. "We can explain."

"Yeah," said Tipp.

"Thing is," the older boy said. "If you're willing to steal, you're probably willing to lie too. So, whatever you got to say, you can just save it."

He ran at Elina and tried to get her in a headlock. Her hat came off and her long hair suddenly billowed out. This caught the boy by surprise. Elina had her head down and was flailing with her arms, and crying.

The boy backed away. He put his hand on his younger brother's chest and they watched Elina as she continued to flail, not realizing that the fight was over before it had begun.

"You're a girl," the older boy said.

"Yeah, that's right," Elina said, sniffing.

"Why aren't you wearing a dress?"

"Because I couldn't find one!" Elina said with a frown, throwing up her arms with frustration. She was practically hysterical. "I'm really sorry we took your clothes without asking. We shouldn't have done it! It's bad! But, we're not thieves, I swear! We'll make it up to you."

"Okay," the older boy said. "It's okay. Do you live in the same building as us?"

"Kind of," Tipp said. "We're staying with Hudson Cavalier. We're his distant relatives." Tipp had a wide grin as he said this.

"The inventor," the younger boy said. "I'm Cecil, by the way."

"I'm Tipp, and this is Elina."

"William," the older boy said. "Pleased to meet you, Elina." He nodded to her and extended his hand. Tipp scowled. The boy was being way too nice to his sister, especially since they were about to punch their lights out just seconds ago.

"Nice to meet you too, William," Elina said, wiping her eyes.

"Listen," William said. "I'm really sorry I pushed you. Maybe we can help you out. Maybe we can help you get a dress."

"What?" Cecil asked, looking at his brother like he'd gone mad. He received an elbow to his chest. "Ow!"

"Why don't we go see my father. He works at the theater. There's always something there that we could find," William said.

"Okay," Elina agreed. "Thanks."

Tipp wasn't sure what was going on, but he was very suspicious of this William character, and wasn't too sure about Cecil either.

The four of them walked over to Broadway and entered a theater through the back door. A rehearsal was going on, and actors were going over their lines.

The children watched from the side of the stage as the actors went through the motions of the play. It wasn't anything Tipp or Elina had ever seen before, and truthfully, it wasn't very interesting. The actors just kept telling each other how much they hated to leave, but that they had to. That war was tearing them apart and that true love would find a way to survive. Oh, the horrors of war! Oh, the sadness of being apart! But, love is the truest bond of all! Blech!

"Father," William whispered to a man who was holding papers that looked like a script in his hands and mouthing the words the actors were speaking. He turned to see the children, and then held his hand up to them.

The actors on the stage continued with the scene, until a director called out for the curtain and clapped.

William and Cecil's father turned and came over to his sons. His face was soaked with sweat. He sat on the edge of the stage. He pulled a kerchief from his pocket and dabbed at his brow with it.

"That director is relentless!" he said.

"Father," William said. "I'd like you to meet our new friends, Tipp and Elina Cavalier. They live in our building."

"He's just so demanding!"

"Do you think it would be an inconvenience to anyone if we looked through costuming for a few extra things for Elina?" William asked.

"And condescending! How can anyone work under these conditions? One certainly can't be expected to be creative in such an environment!"

"Thank you, father," William said, kissing his father on the cheek.

In costuming, Elina found a dress that she absolutely adored. She went behind the screen and tried it on. It fit perfectly! She was able to stuff her cargo pants and t-shirt into her bag. As she emerged from behind the screen she handed the bag to Tipp, as it would have looked awkward with her new outfit.

Tipp found a dandy shirt, jacket and vest that went with his hat quite well. The children looked at themselves in the mirror and then suddenly realized something.

"These are the clothes," Elina said.

"Yeah," Tipp agreed, wide eyed as well. "Crazy."

"What do you think?" Elina said. "Will I get confused for a boy in this?"

"Wow," William said. The orchestra was practicing the musical score to the play now, and William extended his hand. "May I have this dance?"

"Sure!" Elina said excitedly.

The two of them danced to the music. Elina had taken six years of dance lessons. William was quite good. For a boy, that is. It seemed like only a few minutes to Elina before the orchestra stopped mid-note, and the director of the production was yelling at someone and throwing papers and knocking over chairs.

"Thank you," William said, bowing like a gentleman.

"You've got to be kidding me," Cecil said.

"I know, right?" Tipp agreed.

"Get out!" The director was now yelling. "Everyone out! You are all worthless. You should all go home and hang yourselves!" He turned and stormed off, throwing a handful of papers high into the air.

A murmur began after the director had left the room, and everyone began to pack up and go home. The children were stunned by the spectacle of it.

"I guess we should go too," Tipp said.

With the stolen clothing now returned to the rightful

owners, Tipp and Elina prepared to part company with their new friends.

"But what about these clothes," Elina said, indicating the items they had taken from the theater's costuming department.

"Don't worry about it," William said. "We'll sweep floors to pay it off."

"We will?" Cecil asked.

"Sure," William said.

"You have been so nice to us," Elina said. "I wish there was something we could do that you could remember us by."

"Oh, I'll never forget you," William said. "Besides, with you in the building and all."

"But we might have to leave soon," Elina said. "And if we did, and we never got to see each other again, well, it would make me sad."

"Me too," William said.

"Oh, brother," Tipp said.

"You said it," Cecil said.

"Hey, want to see something cool," Tipp asked Cecil, thoroughly disgusted by the spectacle of his sister and William.

"Sure," came the reply.

Tipp slid the computer tablet out and turned it on. Cecil was transfixed. Tipp selected the "videos" icon with his finger and then selected one he knew Cecil would love. It was a sword fighting scene from *John Carter*. Cecil's eyes grew large.

"Boys!" It was William and Cecil's father. "Boys, we must go! They are closing the theater now. Rehearsals are finished. Boys!"

"We need to go, Cecil," William said. He dragged his brother away.

"If I get the chance, maybe I can stop by and say hello, or goodbye, I mean, before I leave," Elina said. "Which apartment are you in?"

"3D," William called, still dragging his speechless brother. "D like our last name, DeMille."

CHAPTER 11

It only took about fifteen minutes for them to locate the building where Nikola and Hudson's lab was on Grand Avenue. By the time they had climbed the four stories their feet hurt and they were exhausted.

Tipp knocked on the door and in just moments, Hudson opened it wide. He was quite surprised to see them, and ushered them in, closing the door behind them.

"Where have you two been?" he asked sharply. "I received your note, but it was not wise for you to go out and about on your own. This can be a dangerous city."

"We're sorry. We got bored and hungry," Tipp said.

"Did you talk with anyone?" Hudson asked.

"Not really," Elina said, *not really* telling the truth.

"Of course you didn't!" A voice that sounded familiar came from a person sitting in a chair not facing them. "You didn't talk to a soul, did you?"

The man stood and turned to face them. It was none other than Mark Twain!

"Well, we talked to a few people," Elina recanted.

"How long did you play your little magic trick for the general public?" Twain asked with a smirk. "Or, did you just play me for my two cents worth? Ah, the charade continues. Brother El was really a sister. All full of intrigue, the two of you."

"We were hungry, we needed money to buy food," Tipp said. "Plus, you said you liked it."

"Oh, indeed I did! But little did I know the two of you were time travelers! My friend Tesla here told me all about it. Quite interesting, indeed. If you would be so kind as to let me take another look at that device you marketed so well on Broadway, I would be much obliged."

"Okay," Elina said. "But the batteries are running low." She handed it over to him and let him play with it for a bit, while Hudson directed them over to a tray on one of the work benches with sliced apples, pears, and cheese. There were also pieces of sliced pepperoni, but it was too spicy for them.

"Huh! Well, I'll be horsewhipped and sent to Timbuktu!" Twain said. "You have a whole library of books on this contraption." He had already figured out how to thumb through pages, and found himself flipping through the bookshelves. Elina had downloaded many free books the first day she had been given the tablet, so she had quite a few of the classics.

"And here it is, bless your heart! The Adventures of Tom Sawyer by yours truly," he said with admiration. "What's this do-hickey do?" He pressed his finger on the screen and nearly dropped the tablet from shock as a female voice began to read the book aloud.

"Well if that just doesn't beat all! This is the most amazing thing I have ever seen in my humble existence on God's green earth," he said, holding it up to his ear. After a few moments, he handed the tablet back to Elina. "If I don't give it up now, I do believe I would never want to at all."

"What are you doing here?" Tipp asked.

"Nikola and I share a fascination of all things technological in nature. When I saw your little Broadway production, I headed straight over here to discuss it with him. Of course, he already knew that of which I was preaching. It would appear that I was proselytizing to the already converted. I decided I would wait an hour or two just so I could have another peek at it. I do believe it was worth it," he said. "Time travel. What an interesting concept."

"Elina, you and your brother shouldn't have wandered off like that," Hudson said. "As long as you are here, I consider you under my care."

"After all, you are relatives, are you not?" Twain asked. "Amazing Cavalier, indeed! Why the resemblance is striking, Hudson! Look at them. They are no doubt your progeny."

"I think we are," Elina spoke up. "Our great-grandfather, is, or I guess, will be your son when he's born in 1922. He lived for ninety-one years and died just two days before we traveled here."

"A son in 1922?" Hudson asked. "Impossible. My wife

Josephine could not possibly give birth in 1922."

"Nothing is impossible, especially in the future," Twain laughed, clapping a hand down on Hudson's shoulder. "Finding out one is going to be a father is always a shock, especially when it's some forty years out of chronology!" He let out a good laugh at that, and even Hudson had to chuckle even as his cheeks reddened .

"Well, I must be off. I have a wife of my own to attend to. Perhaps, we will get a chance to meet again before you depart to your own time, Amazing Cavalier and Sister Elina, is it?" He reached out and shook both of their hands and then turned to exit. "Good-bye, Nikola."

He waited for a reply, but there wasn't one.

"He never says good-bye to me," Twain confided in the children. With that, he left the laboratory.

"Children," Hudson said. "Why don't we go out for a bit of dinner and leave Nikola to continue working. I've arranged to have a mattress delivered here later. You can spend the night in the lab. I believe it will be more comfortable for us all."

"Okay," Tipp said. "Where are we going for dinner?"

"There's a restaurant several blocks away that Nikola and I enjoy immensely. I don't feel like walking, as it's already been a long day. Let's fetch a cab and we can ride uptown for dinner," Hudson said. "Nikola, are you sure you won't be joining us?"

"I cannot," Tesla said. "There's simply too much work to be completed for such frivolities."

"Suit yourself," Hudson said. "Come along children. I will buy you dinner in exchange for stories of the future."

The three of them, family members from opposite ends of the family tree, made their way down from the laboratory and out to the street. Hudson whistled for a cab. A beautiful horse pulling a black cab came to an abrupt stop in front of them.

"Where to, mister?" The driver called down from his seat. He wore a suit and top hat. To the children, it felt, once again, like they were living in a movie.

"Delmonico's," Hudson said, as he helped the children up into the cab.

It was a bumpy ride uptown to Delmonico's Restaurant. The steel springs of the carriage didn't dampen the repeated impacts of the rough, cobblestone road. At first, Tipp and Elina found it to be entertaining, but after just a few blocks, Elina had to put her head out the window, as motion sickness was getting the better of her.

It took several minutes for the feelings of nausea to leave even her after they had arrived at Delmonico's. Once the feeling was gone, she realized how hungry she'd become.

The three of them were shown to a table, and both Tipp and Elina used their proper table manners, putting their cloth napkins in their laps, and retrieving their water glasses for the waiter.

Delmonico's featured fresh steak and potatoes as well

as cooked vegetables. They all ordered the same dish, and then began discussing the future.

"So tell me, what is the future like? Describe it to me," Hudson said as he took a sip of water. He leaned in, ready to listen intently.

"Well, first of all," Elina began. "There's cars and buses and trucks. No one travels by horse and buggy anymore. And the streets are paved, but there's still potholes. But, they try to patch them up. Also, everybody has a radio or MP3 player in their car so they can listen to music. And the clothes are cooler. They are much more comfortable, too. And girls don't have to wear dresses all the time. They can wear whatever they want. Let's see, what else. The buildings are taller, they call them skyscrapers. And there's jet airplanes that can take you all over the world in just a few hours. In fact, our parents just flew to Australia to search for our grandparents, who are missing. But, when we get back, I'm sure they'll be fine. And, we have games. Like, video games. Oh! We have TV. Like, flatscreen TVs that you can watch, like, a hundred different channels on. And movies, you can get movies on demand, whatever you want to watch, you can just download it and watch it." Elina stopped to take a breath and a sip of water.

"Incredible. So, tell me again how you can overlook all of the different rivers and channels? How does that work?" Hudson asked.

"What?" Elina was confused.

"You said you could watch channels. Do people still travel by boat?"

"Yeah," Tipp interjected. "But for fun. You go on cruises in the Caribbean or Alaska. We went on a cruise to Alaska once. It was awesome."

"And we have our own boat too, but we just take it out for fishing, but sometimes down to the Bahamas," Elina added.

"I just can't comprehend all the things I've just heard. Some of the phrases, the terminology escapes me. For instance, what's a T and V?" Hudson asked.

"TV, it's television. It's like movies. You know like the computer tablet, only bigger. And channels are like different programs you get to watch," Tipp said. "Imagine watching a play or musical in a theater, and then getting to get to choose between another play in a different theater in an instant! That's what switching programs is like."

"I believe I understand now," Hudson said, though from the expression on his face, it was obvious he did not. He leaned back, and was quiet for a moment. The children could tell he was lost in thought.

All around them people chattered away, lost in their own discussions. There was talk of politics, corruption, crime, banks, horses, houses, marriages, children, and even the newest gadgets. Both of the children found it interesting that people were generally the same, or at least they had the same concerns.

Finally, the meals arrived. Everything smelled delicious, and the children were ready to dig in.

"Can I be of any further service? Is there anything else at all I can do to make your meal more pleasurable? Perhaps, providing the musicians with a musical request?" the waiter, who was dressed in a sharp white jacket, shirt and bow tie, asked.

"Um, could I get some ketchup?" Tipp asked.

"Ketchup?" The waiter looked confused. "I will see if we have such a thing in the kitchen." He hurried back to the kitchen wearing a worried look on his face.

"They've never heard of ketchup before?" Elina asked in amazement.

"What is ketchup?" Hudson inquired.

"It's like tomato sauce, only, like, with a little bit more zip. I don't know what's in it," Elina said.

"Tomato concentrate from red ripe tomatoes, distilled vinegar, high fructose syrup, corn syrup, salt, spice, onion powder, and then natural flavoring. I'm not sure what the natural flavoring is. I guess that's the secret part that makes it so good," Tipp recited the ingredients to the others. "I like reading the labels on stuff."

The waiter returned with a vexed expression on his face.

"I'm so sorry, young master, but no one in the kitchen has heard of ketchup," the waiter said. "Perhaps if you could explain it a bit I could have some made for you."

Tipp told him the ingredients, and the waiter took them down on his small note pad. He hurried once again back to the kitchen, while the group began eating. Tipp focused on his potatoes and veggies. He just didn't like the taste of meat without ketchup. After several minutes the waiter returned with a small sauce dish with a lumpy red concoction on it.

"I hope this is to your liking," the waiter said as he laid it down on the table. Tipp cut a piece of his steak and dipped it into the lumpy ketchup. He chewed, and stopped, and chewed, and looked like he was really trying to make a fair assessment of the flavor.

"It's not bad," Tipp said. "Not quite as salty, I think, but it's pretty good."

"I'm so pleased you like it," the waiter absolutely beamed. "I shall convey your appreciation to our chef!"

With that the waiter left them to their meals, and they made short work of them. None of them left even a scrap on their plates, as they were so hungry.

"Well, I think it best we return to the laboratory and get you two into bed. Have you any thoughts about what you would like to do tomorrow?" Hudson said as he pushed back his chair and stood. He signed a piece of paper and left it by his plate. Tipp caught sight of it, and it said: Add to the tab of N. Tesla.

"What is there to do?" Elina asked.

"Well, let's see. You could visit the American Museum of Natural History."

"Oh! That would be fun," Elina said, as they walked towards the exit. "We love going there!"

Hudson hailed a cab, and they endured the bumpy ride back to the laboratory. Sure enough, cots had been brought in for the children to sleep. A large curtain had been strung up in a corner so as to provide them with both privacy and darkness. Nikola would continue to work well into the wee hours of the morning.

Tipp and Elina fell asleep dreaming of the day ahead. A day at the museum!

CHAPTER 12

After a light breakfast Tipp and Elina set off for 77th Street and 8th Avenue where the Museum of Natural History stood. They took in the sights and sounds of late 19th century New York. Storekeepers called out their daily specials. Horses clacked hooves against the stones of the road, the trolleys they pulled rolled along rails laid into the streets. With each stop, the trolleys bells rang. People strolled by in their finest apparel, ladies in beautiful dresses, men in top hats and canes, having loud conversations and laughing boisterously.

The children took it all in. What was missing was the honking horns, the jack hammers, the cursing and the screeching tires. There was a peacefulness about it all. The world hadn't been through some of the worst atrocities yet. World War One, World War Two, nuclear weapons, terrorism; all of it was so far off from these people. Tipp and Elina knew what was ahead, and it made them sad to think that such a beautiful world wouldn't last, that eventually it would be ripped apart. Greed and pollution was what was in store for this great city. Violence and sadness. War and misery.

But there was nothing two kids could do about something as big as all of that. They were just kids.

They didn't have any money for a cab or the subway, so they walked up Manhattan Island towards Central Park. It was a beautiful sunny day and the air was fresh and smelled of salt from the Atlantic. There was a strong breeze coming in from the east, blowing all of the smoke from the stacks to the west, back inland, and all the fresh air in from the sea, right over the city.

Time slipped by quickly, and they finally came to the front of the Museum. The tall pillars and the large archway loomed above them. The famous words were chiseled into the building's fascia: TRUTH, KNOWLEDGE, VISION. The words brought comfort to them. They had seen them dozens of times before, stood in this very spot with their parents on many weekends, excitedly waiting to get in and explore the knowledge within.

They entered through the large doors and went immediately to the mammal exhibit. It was one of their favorites. The exhibit was much smaller in 1891 than it was in their own time. The displays were less extravagant, and the lighting was not nearly as bright. There were less children and more adults looking at the exhibits.

Elina and Tipp spent the whole day exploring the Museum, and didn't leave until it closed. It was five o'clock, and they knew there was an hour and a half walk back to the laboratory, so they started on their way. They had become so engrossed in the exhibits they had seen, they had lost all concept of time, and realized that they hadn't eaten since breakfast. This put a little quickening in their step as they wanted to get back to the lab and eat.

As they walked, Tipp saw a sign out of the corner of his eye. He stopped his sister and tugged her down a side street.

"Tipp, I don't want to go down there," she said.

"I just want to see something," Tipp said, pulling her behind him. They walked down the side street to a doorway with a gaslight which illuminated a sign. It read "The Brothers Houdini Featuring the King of Cards and Daring Acts of Escapism!"

"Elina! We have to go in!" Tipp exclaimed.

"Tipp, we don't have any money," Elina said.

"Okay, well, we go back to the lab and beg them for the money, then we come back," Tipp said.

"You and Houdini," Elina said. "I honestly don't understand what you see in it. It's just silly."

"And, I don't understand what you see in pink kitties," Tipp replied.

"Fair enough," Elina said under her breath. "Come on, let's go."

Tipp took note of the street address and they headed back to the laboratory.

By the time they reached the last step of the fourth floor and opened the door to Tesla's lab, their feet were hurting. Hudson and Nikola were still working on the machine. They had many parts laid out on the benches, and they were methodically attaching elements together.

"Back so soon from wasting a day?" Tesla asked.

"We went to the museum. We didn't waste our day," Tipp said.

"There were at least a dozen things you could have done here, helping us! Assisting us! Do you think we are fixing this machine for our health?" Tesla asked. The children were silent.

"I think what Nikola means to say is that since it is your return that hinges on the successful repair of this machine, it would seem that you might wish to show a bit more interest in helping. For example, since you both are owners of small hands, you might be able to reach into cramped enclosures on the machine rather than having us waste time removing components to get to burned out wires," Hudson said.

"So you want us to help?" Elina asked.

Tesla sighed heavily and went back to work. Elina took Tipp aside and they whispered to each other.

"I think they want us to help them with the machine," Elina said.

"But what can we do? We don't know anything about it," Tipp said.

"I know, but maybe they just want us to go get tools and stuff, like when Dad is working on something at home."

"We can do that," Tipp replied.

"Yeah, we can do that, right?" Elina agreed.

"Okay," Elina said to Hudson and Nikola. "What can we do to help?"

"Stay out of the way," Nikola said with a grumble.

There was food left on one of the workbenches, so the children ate the crackers, pepperoni, cheese and fruit that was there. There was plenty, so they were able to eat until they were full. They did as they were asked and stayed out of the way. Every once in awhile, Hudson or Nikola would ask for a certain tool and Elina or Tipp would jump up and run to the workbench to retrieve it, but for the most part the children just sat and watched the men work.

The night grew long, and eventually the children nodded off, laying their heads down on the work bench and going to sleep.

The next few days, the children helped as best they could around the lab. They would fetch tools as asked or run an errand in town to retrieve a part or even lunch. After five days of non stop work, Tesla declared that they had shaved the seventeen days down to ten days. He estimated he could send them home on June 4th. That was just five days away, a Wednesday. He even declared that they had reached a point where they could have Saturday and Sunday off. The following few days would involve hours of precision tests and calibrations, so Tesla preferred to be left alone.

"I want to go see The Houdini Brothers perform, and then a baseball game!" Tipp said.

"What about you, Elina?" Hudson asked.

"I just want to go home," Elina said. She longed for a hot shower, her soft bed and her stuffed animals. "I wouldn't mind going to see a magic show and a baseball game, though."

"Then it's settled," Hudson said. "Tonight, we will have dinner and a show, and tomorrow, my wife Josephine shall join us for a day at the ballpark! She is arriving by train in the morning."

"What are we going to have for dinner?" Tipp asked.

"I thought we would go to Delmonico's again," Hudson suggested. "Unless anyone was opposed to the idea."

"I'm good with that," Tipp said.

"Me too," Elina agreed.

"Let's walk tonight," Hudson said. "The night air is so warm and inviting. Nikola, shall we get anything for you?"

"Nothing!" Tesla called out.

"Suit yourself," Hudson said. They walked down the flights of steps to street level and headed several blocks north to Delmonico's restaurant.

They were shown to a table and given menus. It took just a few moments for the waiter to arrive with a pitcher to fill their water glasses.

"Ah, young master! You will be pleased to know, we have just received our first order direct from Pittsburgh of genuine Heinz brand ketchup. I think it will be to your liking," the waiter said. This brought a smile to Tipp's face.

They ordered their food, and after just a few minutes, it arrived, smelling delicious. True to his word, the waiter produced a bottle of ketchup. Tipp didn't hesitate to pour it onto his steak.

By the time they finished their meals, they rose to leave, and Hudson signed the meal to his tab. It was six o'clock, and they had an hour to walk the five blocks to where The Brothers Houdini would be performing. They strolled up the avenue, taking their time, enjoying the night air. The gaslights in the street lamps made the shadows dance on the sidewalks. It gave the city an eerie feeling. It was the perfect aura for an evening with the Brothers Houdini.

They arrived at the tiny, off-Broadway theater twenty minutes before the show started. Hudson paid their admission, and they were shown to their seats. Only a handful of people were in the audience along with the Cavaliers.

A well worn, burgundy curtain obscured the stage, and every so often it moved, as people were busy setting things up behind it. A few more audience members trickled in, and the lights were lowered in the auditorium. The curtains were drawn open and a young man addressed the audience.

"Ladies and gentlemen, prepare yourselves for amazing feats that will thrill and baffle you! You will scarcely believe your eyes as the King of Cards, Harry Houdini, himself will perform the impossible, and then the Brothers Houdini will perform feats of escapism that defy logic and the laws of physics. Prepare to be shocked and amazed by the Brothers Houdini!" A smattering of applause followed.

The announcer left the stage and a very young Harry Houdini entered stage right. He produced a deck of cards and showed it to the audience. He fanned them so the audience could see all of the suits. He pulled the ace of spades from the deck and slid the single card into his suit breast pocket. The rest of the deck was then shuffled.

"May I have a volunteer?" Houdini asked.

Tipp's hand shot up. "Me!" He cried out. A smirk came across Houdini's face.

"You, young man, you seem more than willing," Houdini said. Tipp bolted from his chair and up the two steps onto the stage.

"Please, select a card," Houdini said. Tipp did as he was told. "Now, show it to the rest of the audience."

Tipp held up the card. It was the ace of spades! The crowd reacted with genuine surprise and applause. Whispers of "how did he do that" were murmured throughout the audience.

"Thank you, young man," Houdini said. Tipp handed the ace back to him. "Oh, you may keep it." This gave Tipp a smile from ear to ear. He clutched it close as he returned to his seat.

Houdini performed several other card tricks. He even made a card seem to rise from his breast pocket on its own. This elicited a cry from someone in the audience that "he has a demon!" Others in the audience reacted with laughter and derision at this. Houdini stopped the act when this was said.

"Please, let me assure you. The things that you see are not of the supernatural. They are merely illusions. Tricks. Please refrain from making such spectacular accusations of a supernatural nature." There were snickers and laughter after he made the declaration. Houdini continued with several more tricks, took a bow, and the curtains closed to applause.

The announcer returned to the stage and introduced the next act, The Brothers Houdini performing feats of escapism. The curtains opened again, and Harry Houdini and his brother were chained in stocks, their heads and hands bound fast.

"As you can see," Harry called out to the crowd. "We are bound fast by these stocks. They are fastened by padlocks. The same padlocks used by the New York Police Department when securing prisoners for transport between prisons. We will liberate ourselves from these in less than one minute! Does someone have a pocket watch?"

A member of the audience raised a hand.

"Sir, if you could come up on stage and keep time for us," Houdini said. The man stood and walked up on stage. "Remember, one minute's time, sir."

The announcer brought out a black cloak and draped it over the brothers, as the time keeper made note of the time. There was barely any movement at all under the cloak. It looked as if the Brothers Houdini were just standing there!

After barely ten seconds, the stocks and locks dropped

to the ground and the Brothers Houdini whipped off the black cloak and stood up, completely freed from the bonds.

The audience clapped wildly. The brothers took a bow. They went on to perform several other escapist tricks. One involved handcuffs in a bag that seemed to take only a moment to unlock. Another was the classic escapist routine which involved Harry Houdini being secured in a straight jacket and then being placed into a large canvas bag. It took Houdini several minutes to extract himself from the straight jacket, and when he finally emerged from the canvas bag, he was sweating profusely and his face was flushed. He smiled to the audience, but he had a very concerned look on his face.

All in all, the Cavaliers were pleased with the performance, especially Tipp. The Brothers Houdini took the final curtain around eight-thirty, with a dramatic bow. The audience filed out, with mostly positive comments. It was no wonder that Houdini was destined to become the most famous escape artist of all time. Word of mouth was going to be very good for the performer.

Tipp wanted to wait and see if he could meet the escapist. Hudson indulged the boy, and they headed up to the stage door to inquire about Houdini. The stage hand, who looked like he was about thirteen, said he would check to see if Houdini would meet them. Moments later, the great Harry Houdini stepped out from the stage door, mopping his brow with a towel. He had removed his jacket and loosened his collar.

"Why, if it isn't my assistant!" Houdini said. "I suppose

my gratitude is in order. You helped launch a great evening for me. The comments from the audience were all very positive."

"You were awesome!" Tipp said.

"Awe-some," Houdini echoed. He pulled a pad and pencil from his pocket. "You don't mind if I use that on our next billing, do you? It has a very nice ring to it. So, what is your name?"

"Tipp Cavalier, and this is my sister Elina, and this is Hudson. He works for Nikola Tesla," Tipp said.

"Ah, the inventor! I've heard of him. I'm very intrigued by some of Tesla's inventions," Houdini said.

"Why didn't you do your best trick?" Tipp asked.

"What's my best trick?" Houdini asked, furrowing his brow.

"The drowning man trick. Where you're suspended upside down in a tank of water all chained up and you have to escape. That's the trick that made you famous," Tipp said.

"Hmm," Houdini thought for a moment. "I've never heard of such a trick. You have quite an imagination for a young boy. I would imagine that if an escapist could perform such a feat he would become quite famous indeed. Quite famous. I thank you very much for coming, but I must go. Thank you again Cavaliers. I hope you did enjoy yourselves."

"Yes we did!" Tipp said.

"We had a great time," Elina added.

"A pleasure to meet you, sir," Hudson said.

The three Cavaliers left the small theater and headed back to the laboratory. It was getting late and tomorrow was going to be just as busy a day. Tipp was still floating with his head in the clouds. He had met the real Harry Houdini!

When they had returned to the fourth floor lab, Tesla was working quietly on some computations. The machine looked as if he had completed the final assembly. The children went behind the curtain and readied themselves for bed. Hudson excused himself and headed back to his apartment just a few blocks away.

"Elina," Tipp whispered as they lay there waiting to fall asleep.

"What?"

"Are you glad we came back in time?"

"Yeah, kind of," she said.

"Do you want to go back?"

"Yeah, I do."

"Me too."

"Do you miss mom and dad?"

"Yeah," Tipp said. "Do you?"

"Yeah."

"But, I wish they could be here, that they could see all the stuff we're seeing, too."

"I know what you mean," Elina said.

"Do you think we'll ever get home?"

"I don't know."

"I hope so," Tipp said.

"Me too. Go to sleep."

CHAPTER 13

It was another beautiful sunny day in New York City. The children awoke to a knock at the door. Tesla answered it and took delivery of the food from a young boy who looked to be no older than Tipp.

"You realize," Nikola said. "That even on a day off, if you two are to eat, you must earn your keep. After breakfast I expect you to sweep the floor and dust the furniture. Also, the windows and the lamp glasses must all be cleaned. I need light for my work."

They weren't unaccustomed to chores. They had been working hard all week. Plus, they had been taught a strong work ethic by their parents, despite their familial wealth.

"You should work harder because of what we have, not less," their father would say. "And be generous to those without, if they are willing to work." Work was an important part of the lessons they received. Tipp was responsible for keeping his room clean, taking the trash down to the dumpster and tidying up before Mrs. Backnackerson arrived to start the heavy cleaning. Elina helped around the house as well, though she didn't really have any assignments. She just naturally seemed to pitch in and help out. She preferred to have a neat and tidy room, whereas Tipp needed a bit more prodding.

"Okay," the children agreed. They were too hungry to argue.

"Where's Hudson," Tipp asked.

"He is at the rail station," Tesla said simply. Tesla set back to his work, fine tuning the machine that had brought the children to 1891.

When their meals were finished, the children followed Tesla's instructions, beginning their chores. Tipp swept the floor with a broom and dust pan, dumping the scraps into a metal can. He kept at the task until the floor was in pristine condition.

Elina first washed out the lamp glass that protected the gaslights from blowing out. They had been blackened by the flickering flames and therefore allowed less light to show out into the room. Elina's small hands could fit all the way into the glass housings, and she was able to polish the soot off, leaving them sparkling and clear. There were eight gaslights in all, including the chandelier which she could only reach by using a step ladder. Once she had finished that task, she washed what she could of the windows. There was no way for her to reach the outside without endangering herself, but she made the insides of the windows spotless.

Tipp lugged the metal garbage can down the four flights of stairs out to the street, where he was instructed by Tesla to dump it in the alley, after all, it was just dirt. Tipp did as he was instructed, but he felt funny about just dumping a pile of dirt there, so he spread it out a bit with his shoes.

By the time they had finished dusting the furniture, the door to the laboratory opened and in walked Hudson, with a beautiful woman on his arm. She wore an ankle length dress with a blouse that went up to her neck. Her leather shoes buttoned up the side, and caught Elina's attention immediately.

"Children, may I present to you my wife, Josephine Cavalier," Hudson said. She smiled sweetly at the children and approached them. She gave each of them a big hug, and for the children, it was exactly what they needed.

"I am so very pleased to meet both of you," Josephine said. "And you may call me Josie. When I received the wire from Hudson about your incredible appearance, I arranged to return from my parents' vacation home in the Catskills by train. I came as fast as I could. I have so many questions about the future!"

"Now, now, Josie. I've already interrogated them enough. We have baseball to attend to. There will be time enough to discuss the future to your heart's content. We must be going if we don't want to miss the first pitch," Hudson said.

"Alright, my dear. But let me first take a photograph of you and the children by the machine. We shall keep it for posterity. It's not everyday that you meet time travelers. My friend Henry Clay has just received a patent for this design," Josephine said. "It will revolutionize photographs." She set, what looked like, a small suitcase on a wooden tripod. She unhooked a clasp and lowered a side. A lens telescoped out. She made a few adjustments to the lens, and prepared for the photograph. In just a few moments she was ready.

"Smile," Josephine instructed. She slid a shutter open quickly and then closed again. She pulled the dry plate from the back of the camera and slid it into the holder on the back of the unit. She then closed up the case, re-engaged the clasp, folded up the tripod and set the entire unit in the corner of the laboratory.

"There, we are ready to go. I can process the plate later," Josephine said.

"Nikola, are you sure you would not like to join us?" Hudson asked. "You have been working like a madman. A day in the sun would do you well, my friend."

"I'm fine, dear Hudson. I shall press on with the work while you partake of the games and recreations of those heady Brooklynites!" Nikola bellowed from behind the machine. "Don't feel guilty in the least about leaving me behind with all of this work to do."

"Tesla, it's Saturday. The weekends are my own, unless you would like to increase my salary," Hudson countered.

"Enjoy the baseball game, and let that be the end of any insane notions of increased salary," Nikola said.

The four of them, Hudson, Josie, Elina and Tipp, descended to street level of the Grand Street laboratory and hailed a horse drawn cab for their ride to Brooklyn. Once again the children were able to cross the Brooklyn Bridge. It was so strange to have crossed it so many times that they had a feeling of familiarity and normalcy. And yet, here they were, in an open carriage, in late 19th century clothing, riding with their great-great-grandfather; it was anything but familiar and normal!

Hudson had selected an open carriage for their ride, so they were able to take in the entirety of the city as it stood in 1891. The rising smoke from the stacks, the constant clopping sound of hooves on cobblestone, and the smells - sometimes pungent and chokingly awful, other times delightful and mouth watering.

After a short ride through Brooklyn, they finally arrived at Eastern Park. A few hundred people were still streaming into the small stadium. Hudson paid the carriage driver and then stepped down to the street, assisting Josie after him. The children bundled out of the carriage and started towards the stadium when they were grabbed from behind by Hudson.

"Look out!" He yelled.

A trolley went rolling by, a pair of horses pulling it in full trot. If Hudson hadn't grabbed Tipp he very well could have been run down. It wasn't the only trolley they had to dodge as they headed in to watch the baseball game.

"Tipp, you need to be more careful. That's the second horse that's almost run you over," Elina said, using her motherly tone.

"I know!" Tipp shot back.

"I'm just trying to help, you don't have to be so touchy."

"I'm not being touchy. You're being bossy," Tipp said.

"Children," Josie cut in. "I hope you don't plan on acting like a couple of unruly little puppies the whole day. I shall have to roll up a newspaper and bop you both on the noses."

"Sorry," Tipp replied.

"Elina, apologize to your brother," Josie instructed.

"But, I didn't do anything," she complained.

"Tut, tut. No arguments. Apologize," Josie insisted.

"Sorry, Tipp." It was less than an enthusiastic apology, but the small fray that had begun to boil up subsided. The group purchased their tickets to the double header baseball game and headed towards the entrance to Eastern Park to watch the game.

"Mmm. I smell popcorn and roasted peanuts," Elina said. Parked outside of the entrance was a horse drawn cart with the name C. Cretors and Company on its side. It advertised buttered popcorn, roasted peanuts and fine chocolates.

"Oh, could we get something?" Josie asked. "You know how much I just adore the new popped corn."

"But it's a nickel," Hudson protested. The look from his wife, however, ended the protest and he entered the line for the snacks. After just a few moments each of the children had a bag of popcorn, while Hudson held a paper cone full of roasted peanuts. They filed into the ballpark, as it was drawing close to the first pitch.

Eastern Park was a fairly small baseball park compared

to what Elina and Tipp were used to in 2013. The new Yankee Stadium was huge, as was Citi Park Stadium where the New York Mets played. The seats here were just long benches where everyone squeezed in together. Nothing like the box seats or luxury suites from where they usually watched games. People had come out to the game outfitted in suits with top hats or bowlers. Many of the women carried parasols or large hats which matched their dresses.

The players took the field, to the applause of the crowd. They were in white and none of them had numbers or names on their jerseys. Their caps had blue stripes and barely-there brims. Many of them had grand, handle bar mustaches. They reminded the children of Sullo.

The players trotted out to their positions in the field, and the pitcher threw a couple of practice pitches to the catcher. The umpire wore a black jacket, and was smoking a cigar.

"Play ball!" the umpire bellowed.

Hudson had purchased a scorecard which had the lineup for the day as well as many advertisements from all over Brooklyn. The cover featured an illustration of a Groomsman ballplayer in uniform and fancy scripted text that read "Brooklyn Grooms." Inside was a list of all the players for the Grooms, a rubber stamp of the Pirates logo, and a blank scorecard. For Tipp, it was as if he had received a family heirloom, a priceless piece of jewelry. He handled it carefully, not wanting to crease it. Hudson fished a small pencil from his vest pocket and handed it to Tipp.

"I assume, you know how to score a game," Hudson said.

"You bet I do!"

"Then, I would be honored if you kept score of this game for me. I'd like to keep it as a memento of your visit to our time," Hudson said. Tipp wasn't sure if he really meant it or if he was just trying to be positive about their return to 2013. Whatever the case, Tipp loved to record baseball scores, so he was more than happy to oblige. Though he was a bit disappointed that he wouldn't be able to keep the scorecard.

Tom Lovett was on the mound for the Grooms. He was warming up, throwing the ball in to Tom Kinslow, the catcher. The rest of the team was Dave Foutz 1B, Hub Collins 2B, George Pinkney 3B, John Ward SS, Darby O'Brien LF, Mike Griffin CF and Oyster Burns RF. Adonis Terry was going to be pitching the second game of the double header.

The Pirates' lineup was there as well, but they spelled Pittsburgh wrong. They had left off the "h" at the end. Tipp wondered if it was a mistake, but he saw they spelled it wrong on the jerseys as well. Pud Galvin was the pitcher for the Pirates, with Connie Mack catching. The rest of the lineup was: Jake Beckley 1B, Lou Biefbauer 2B, Charlie Reilly 3B, Frank Shugart SS, Pete Browning LF, Ned Hanlon CF, Fred Carroll RF. Mark Baldwin was scheduled to pitch the second game. Tipp knew that this was an era when pitchers were expected to pitch the whole game. They didn't have relievers or closers. He was going to have to pay attention to all of the little differences between the game as he knew it and how they were playing it here in 1891.

"Did you know," Hudson said as he cracked open a peanut. "That the this is the first year Pittsburg is calling themselves the Pirates? They have always been the Pittsburg Alleghenys. They swiped Lou Bierbauer, the second baseman, from Philadelphia. They were called Pirates by the Philly newspapers. Well the owners thought they would embrace that notion. They decided to officially call themselves the Pittsburg Pirates this year."

"That's cool," Tipp said. Hudson looked at the boy with some question as to whether "cool" was a good thing or bad.

A batter from the Pittsburg Pirates walked up to the home plate, and swung the bat several times in preparation. According to the lineup card, it was Jake Beckley. Tipp looked at the bat, and thought it looked peculiar. It looked as if there was a flat side to it. The pitch was thrown, and with an audible crack, the ball leapt into the air and landed fair in right-center field. Oyster Burns scooped it up bare handed and threw it in to Hub Collins at second base. Beckley was safe at first base. There was a smattering of applause, some boo's, but mostly chatter amongst the on-lookers.

"They really aren't doing so well this year," Hudson

said, cracking another peanut shell between thumb and forefinger and popping the enclosed nuts into his mouth. "Last year they were the champions of the league. This year, they've only managed to win eleven of the last thirty games. I keep up with baseball. I usually try to see a few games every season."

The next batter for Pittsburg, Fred Carroll, the right fielder, didn't have to wait long before he hit a double to left field and brought home Beckley. Collective groans came from the crowd, along with whistles and jeers. It was going to be a long day for the Grooms' pitcher, Lovett.

Without commercial breaks, the game moved along quickly. The Pirates' bats were hot, and Lovett didn't have much of a pitching arsenal. He gave up seven runs. The Grooms couldn't figure out Galvin's pitches at all. They were only able to score one run, though they stranded four runners on the bases.

There was a half-hour intermission between games, which was fine with the children, as the wooden benches were hard on one's backside. After they milled about, used the rest rooms, and purchased more popcorn and peanuts, it was time for the next game to start. The umpire bellowed the "play ball" call. And the Grooms' new pitcher, Adonis Terry threw the first pitch.

He had some fire behind his throws. It wasn't like watching the major league pitchers from 2013, but Terry was good. He would get the ball back from the catcher, lift his leg and throw. Strike! He threw like a pitching machine. The Pirates couldn't hit him!

Oyster Burns hit a two run double in the fourth inning, and Terry helped out his own cause by adding the final run in the seventh inning with a single. The Grooms won 5-0 in eight and a half innings. The Cavaliers were all happy. It had been a great day of baseball.

By the time the games had come to their full conclusion, both the children and the adults were exhausted. They dodged the trolleys by the stadium, walked several blocks to stretch their legs, then found a cab that was willing to take them back to Manhattan.

The ride, though bumpy, was enough to lull the children into sleepiness, especially after being in the sun all day. It was an uneventful trip back to the laboratory on Grand Street. As the carriage drew to a stop, the driver turned and gave the amount of the ride for the four of them. Josie gasped, but Hudson drew out his change purse and handed over the requested amount.

"I'm sure it seems like a pittance by your standards," Hudson said to the children. "But that was nearly a day's pay for most people these days. Fortunately, Mr. Tesla is very generous with me, despite the charades he likes to play."

"But really, Hudson. We could have walked. It would only have taken an hour or so," Josie persisted.

"We shall let it lie, Josephine. It's not an extravagance we partake in regularly, so we should not pay it more than usual concern," Hudson said. "Now, children. Should we see the progress of Nikola?"

"Yeah!" came the cry in unison. With the day's activities, they had almost forgotten about the work Tesla was doing on the machine that would take them home.

They climbed the four flights of stairs, once again, to the laboratory, and Hudson opened the door to let them all in. The children filed in behind Josie. They stopped short, and Hudson had to crane his neck to see over them and eye what all the fuss was about.

"Nikola! What has happened?" Hudson cried out.

CHAPTER 14

Hudson, Josie, Elina and Tipp all stood just inside the door to Nikola Tesla's Grand Street laboratory on the fourth floor. What they saw before them shocked them to their very core.

Tesla was standing in the center of the room with a broom handle held like one would wield a broad sword, two handed and out away from his body. On the floor were two men, both badly burned and apparently dead. The machine was winding down, as if it had been recently used. It didn't look damaged, but there wasn't much light, so it was difficult to tell. What they could see all about the room, however, were, what looked like, claw marks on the floors and walls. Also, the windows that were overlooking Grand Street had been completely smashed out.

Closer to the machine was something laying on the ground. It looked like a child, roughly the same size as Tipp, but as Hudson drew closer, he could see it wasn't a child at all, but some sort of monster. Something completely alien to him.

"Josie, take the children away," Hudson said immediately.

"I want to see what happened," Tipp argued.

"Me too," Elina said.

"Children, it's not safe. Go to my apartment. Nikola and I will be along as soon as we can to tell you everything," Hudson said. He walked over and put a hand on his friend's shoulder. Tesla didn't flinch. He simply lowered the broom handle and then let it slip to the floor.

Josie did as she was asked, and bustled the children back down to the street and over to Hudson's apartment. Though they had given some resistance, both children were content not to be in the room with the dead men. It was the first time either of them had seen a real dead body.

"Children, I need you to get right to bed and get your rest. I'm not sure what has happened, but we may not have the luxury of rest over the next few days," Josie said.

The children didn't reply. Their situation had seemed to take a very serious and ominous turn. They had seen the look in Tesla's eyes when they had first come into the room. His eyes held a mixture of fear, panic and wonderment. They looked almost crazed. He seemed to snap out of it once Hudson began to talk, but something had rattled him right down to his toes. Elina and Tipp wanted to know what it was. They also wanted to know what had made all the scratches in the laboratory. It was a mystery.

Obediently, they made their way into bed. Josie reclined on the couch and crossed her arms. She was going to wait up for her husband.

At first, the children found it difficult to sleep. The day had been so busy and had ended with such a shock that it felt like they would never be able to sleep. Once they did finally nod off, both of them had strange dreams. The dreams would fade away with the morning light, but neither of them had a restful slumber.

When they were awakened by Josie, they both wanted to stay in bed. Josie was persistent, and she got them moving.

"Hudson never came home last night," Josie said. "I don't mean to leave you two here while I check on him. I believe something foul is afoot, and I think it unsafe for you to be out of my sight."

The children got out of bed and groggily began to change into their 19th century clothing.

"No, we haven't the time," Josie said. "Just put on one of Hudson's long coats over your future clothes."

The children pulled on one of his coats each and buttoned them closed over their 2013 clothing. Elina grabbed her computer tablet bag and she slung it over her shoulder as they left the apartment.

The doorman saw them coming down the stairs and immediately stood to confront them.

"Hey, what are you two doing back in here," he barked. He came from behind his desk and poked a finger at Tipp, who was still rubbing the sleep from his eyes.

"Barkley, really!" Josie said. "They are under mine and my husband's care. You should pay them the same level of respect as you would either one of us."

"Mrs. Cavalier, I didn't know. They came running through here in such a rambunctious manner the other day I would never have guessed they were your children, what with you and Mr. Cavalier being so civilized."

"I did not say they were my children, I said they were in my care. Do pay attention, Barkley. Now, would you kindly get the door?" Josie strode forward with her nose held high. The children followed.

"Barkley, like a dog?" Tipp asked.

The doorman pretended like he was going to lunge for the boy. Tipp didn't wait around to find out if he would follow through with the feign. He ran to catch up to Josie and his sister.

They were only into their walk for but a few minutes when they realized something was wrong. The smell of acrid smoke was in the air. Not the smoke of manufacturing or a wood stove, but of something being ablaze that shouldn't be. Black plumes bellowed up into the air just a few blocks away, and the sounds of men shouting and fire bells clanging echoed off the cobblestone streets and brick buildings.

"What is going on?" Elina asked.

"I'm not sure," Josie replied. People were rushing about, as if some great panic had descended on the city. Children were being pulled indoors, and owners were closing their shops. Josie and the children began to notice that some of the windows in the buildings had been broken out, and there were strange things strewn about. A wooden chair lay on its side in the center of the street, a dress maker's dummy was discarded askew against the curb. Debris of all sort was littering the streets and sidewalks as they approached the Grand Street laboratory. It was as if things had been tossed from the windows of the buildings or had been left there by people fleeing.

They started to see small fires in different locations, some coming from within the buildings. It was as if a battle had taken place, and they were walking through the ruins. Suddenly a driver-less carriage pulled by a team of horses rumbled down the street, the horses in a panic. Dogs howled in the distance. Women screamed and men called out in agony. Then there was a noise that sounded like it was a living creature, but it was a noise that none of them had ever heard before. It was unsettling and made the hair on the back of their necks stand on end. A howl that changed to a shriek.

The winds shifted and smoke began to obscure their view. Whereas just moments before they could clearly see the length of the street, they could now scarcely see three feet in front of their faces. The smoke stung their eyes and made them cough and choke.

"This is madness, what is happening?" Josie said out loud, a quiver in her voice.

"Josie!" It was Hudson! He ran through the smoke and embraced her, kissing her on the lips. His face was streaked with soot, and his hair had been singed. His clothing was disheveled and torn in places, as if he had been involved in a struggle.

"What has happened?" Josie said, short of breath from the passionate kiss as well as the smoke.

"Something terrible," he said. "Come with me to the laboratory and I will explain. Tesla is working feverishly to repair and recalibrate the machine so we can send you back and then destroy it."

"But if you destroy it then it won't be there in 2013 for us to use!" Tipp said.

It gave Hudson pause. They could tell he was working out the mechanics of Tipp's theory in his mind, and trying to find a solution around it.

"So be it, but it cannot be used again by anyone else!" Hudson replied. "Come everyone, to the laboratory!"

They raced through the growing destruction as fast as their legs could carry them. The sound of breaking glass and splintering wood seemed to surround them. Men called out for assistance, gunfire started to echo with regularity. There was a call to arms.

"Get your guns!"

"Get your guns!"

"To arms!"

The cries were now raining down from the buildings, even as shots began to fire all around them.

"Quickly, everyone!" Hudson called to them as the gunfire increased. The children saw quick moving shadows in the smoke, darting here and there.

Without warning, there was an explosion behind

them! They felt the heat of it against their backs, but they had reached the laboratory and ducked inside. Hudson barred the door and they headed up the stairs.

"What is going on?" Josie yelled. The noise from outdoors was still finding its way inside the brick building. Another explosion rumbled outside and shook the building. "Is it war? Are we under attack?"

"We must get up to the laboratory!" Hudson yelled.

"I'm scared!" Elina called out to her brother. "I think it's terrorists."

"I'm scared, too," Tipp replied. Something terrible was going on. It was like an army was attacking or there was a riot or something. The children had watched riots on TV after that big storm had hit and there was no gasoline and they were scary. They were safe in their apartment, but Manhattan was dangerous for a week. Schools were closed and business was shut down. But they weren't safely in their apartment in Brooklyn with their parents. They were in 1891 in a city that had gone mad and was beginning to burn to the ground.

"Tesla! The children, I have them!" Hudson said as he burst into the laboratory. Nikola looked up from the machine. The bodies of the men from the previous night were now gone, and there was some order restored to the lab.

"I'm almost done, the machine is almost complete," Tesla said. "I'm setting the final calibrations now. We must make certain that they are properly recorded so the machine in 2013 is set properly as well. Any miscalculation could send them into oblivion, or worse, between dimensions!"

"We've discovered a way to turn on the other doorway," Hudson explained. "The key is having the machines set to the same power and frequency. If they are set to a different frequency, the doorway won't open, or it may open another doorway which we don't want to open."

"Is that what happened?" Tipp asked. "Did the machine open a doorway to someplace different than the one in Great Grandpa Dickie's basement? Someplace bad?"

"Yes. Yes, that's what happened. It's horrible, but we must get you back. If we don't do it now, I fear we may never be able to."

"But, how can you make sure that the frequency and power are at the right settings on the other side?" Elina asked.

"We are in the past, that machine is in the future. That means we can leave information for someone in that moment in time that will give them the instructions on how to set the machine, how to tune it to match this machine's setting," Tesla spoke to them now. "They will then open that side of the portal to match ours, creating a tunnel through space and time, a connection that takes only a moment to experience, but can transport you back to 2013."

"Whoa," Tipp said.

"But how can you make sure that someone will be there? That they will know what to do?" Elina asked.

"Details, details," Tesla said, making more adjustments to the machine.

"I will make sure," Hudson said. "I promise, upon my life."

Tesla had been shoveling coal into the stove, stoking the flames. This boiled the water to create the steam, which would turn the turbine to create the electricity. The whirring hum began to fill their ears. There was a whine and crackle of electricity. The round framework of the Tesla portal began to illuminate. Tesla looked over the equipment, he made note of the settings and then handed a small piece of paper to Hudson. Tesla turned dials, releasing more and more electricity into the machine as the turbine increased speed and the voltage grew.

"Any moment now, children," Tesla said. "Get ready."

The noise from outside on the street suddenly sounded as if it were coming into the building. Hudson put the piece of paper into his jacket pocket and ran to the door, locking it. He grabbed a chair and braced it up under the door handle. He pulled out a pistol from his pocket.

"Tesla, hurry!"

"Any moment," Nikola said above the noise of the machine. The hum was now deafening, and the children could feel it in their chests. Electricity sprang from the machine. It crackled blue and white as a small round portal began to open at the center of the machine's round metal frame work.

There was scratching and pounding at the door.

Hudson braced his shoulder against it, but it was starting to give. The frame around the door was cracking.

"Hurry!"

"There!" Tesla shouted. The portal connected. The children could see the basement of their great-grandfather's mansion in the St. Lawrence river.

"Go! Now! Go!" Hudson yelled. The door broke away and he was knocked to the floor. What came through the door was like a nightmare.

A tall, yellowish-gray creature, that looked like a man, strode through the shattered door frame. He looked like a man, but he was not. His head was bald, and he did not have a nose nor ears. His eyes were grossly enlarged, and his teeth were jagged and long. His skin was mottled, with darker spots, and he wore a robe that was a deep, dark purple. He wasn't the only one to come through the door, however.

Small, more yellowish skinned creatures, which looked like miniature versions of the purple robed being flowed into the room. They had claws on their hands and feet, and wore only what looked like brown loin cloths hanging around their waists. They had gray and black tattoos all over their bodies.

The children, were able to take this all in with widened eyes in just a moment. Without a moment to spare, they were grabbed by Nikola Tesla and tossed, one after the other, through the portal.

They experienced a blue-white flash. For a moment,

it seemed as if they were flying through the stars. Then, Elina and Tipp flew into the basement room where they had first encountered the machine. They landed in a pile on the floor, and it took a moment for them to realize where they were.

Tipp was the first to get to his feet. He looked back at the machine as the portal began to close. Tesla was looking at them, but it was as if he were looking through a thick foggy haze of blue-white static. The portal slowly contracted, the Tesla connection was closing. The great scientist and inventor raised his hand in a wave, and Tipp returned the gesture.

In a flash, one of the yellow creatures launched at Tesla, but the inventor moved with great agility. The yellow creature burst through the portal and landed at Tipp's feet.

The portal closed, and the machine began to wind down to a stop. The room became dark.

CHAPTER 15

"Elina. Tipp." The voice came from the darkness. It sounded familiar to their ears, but they also had the feeling like it was impossible to be hearing that voice again.

The dim lights clicked on, and the children stood face to face with Great Grandpa Dickie.

"Children!" He shouted with joy and hugged them both. The two children hugged him back, and began to cry. He hugged them even tighter.

"But, you're dead!" Elina cried. "You died."

"We have so much to talk about," Great Grandpa Dickie said. "Come now, let's go back upstairs."

"But, the monster!" Tipp said. "A monster came through the portal!"

Great Grandpa Dickie set the children down and looked around the room. He carried a big flashlight, and he shined the beam into the dark corners. There was nothing there.

"Let's go," Dickie said. They followed him up the stairs, and he seemed to be able to walk much better than they remembered. He did not carry a cane, nor did it appear that he needed it. He bounded up the stairs, two at a time.

The finely furnished mansion that they remembered was not what they stepped into when they came up from the basement. The mansion was a run down, dilapidated mess. The corners of the ceiling and the chandelier was thick with cobwebs. The floor was filthy, and trash was strewn about. Spray paint covered the walls. Messages in different languages had been painted by an untalented hand in many different, dripping colors.

"What happened here?" Elina asked.

"I can explain," Dickie said. "I will tell you everything once we get to the library."

It was horrific seeing the home in such a condition. It was run down, windows broken, staircase crumbling. Doors ripped off their hinges, floor boards torn up. It was like a bad dream.

"Here," Dickie said. He stood in front of a large steel door with a big round handle, like a car's steering wheel, right in the center. He produced a large steel key from his pocket and slid it into an equally large lock. He turned the key with some force, then cranked the wheel. There was a loud clicking noise and the large steel door opened. "Hurry inside now. Hurry children!"

A screeching noise was growing outside, like a thousand crows in the sky, cawing in unison. It grew closer and closer, even as it grew in volume. Elina and Tipp ran into the room, followed by Dickie, who slammed the steel door shut and spun the wheel, locking it tight. The noise they had heard was now blocked, and they gave a sigh of relief.

"Would you kids like something to drink?" Dickie asked. He walked across the room to a refrigerator and retrieved several cans of soda. He handed one to each of the children. They popped the tops and slurped at the fizzy beverages.

"So, how was 1891?" Dickie asked.

"How did you know?" Elina questioned.

"There's quite a bit that I have to tell you. Why don't you sit down and make yourselves comfortable," Dickie said. "What I'm about to tell you may scare you, but let me assure you that everything is going to be alright."

He sat in the high backed chair and crossed his legs as he sipped on his soda. He was very different than they remembered him, much younger, but also a bit less refined.

"I can see it on your faces, I'm younger than you remember. Well, it makes sense. This is not 2013," Dickie said.

"What year is it?" Tipp asked.

"It's the year 1984," Dickie said. "The world is not as you remember it from your history books in 2013. The world is in a state of continuous war against the Emperor. His forces are much stronger than they've ever been, and no one is safe from his machines. They are smaller and faster than they once were, but we're safe in here. They can't get through the steel doors. In fact, this entire chamber is like a big steel box. The metal is hidden behind the walls. The Emperor knows that a Tesla portal exists someplace in the world, but he can't find it. He knows one exists because he saw how it worked back in 1891. He saw you children go through it in Tesla's laboratory. And he and his soldiers came through the very same one when Thomas Edison's men played with the dials and switched it on."

"The alien creature?" Elina asked. "He becomes an Emperor?"

"Yes," Dickie said. "It's amazing how quick it all was."

"But he had a machine, a portal. It's the same machine that brought us here," Tipp said. "The one in the basement, right? It's the same one we came through."

"No, it's not. Tesla had seen what had come through the portal the night that Thomas Edison's men had turned it on without him. They were spies sent by Edison to see what Tesla was working on. What they had done instead was open a portal to another dimension. They allowed the Emperor and his army flow into the streets of New York. Tesla destroyed his portal machine right after you used it," Dickie said.

"Then where did the machine in the basement come from?" Tipp asked.

"I built it," Dickie said. "The note that Tesla gave my father, it was the location of the complete record of his work. My father escaped with Josie, even as the Emperor captured Tesla. He tried to make him give up the secret to his machine, but Nikola refused. He took it with him to his grave. My father hid from the Emperor. He and Josie located Tesla's safe and took its contents. They built this house and my father began building another machine according to Tesla's specifications. They had three children together before Josie died. My father remarried, and I was born in 1922, when my father was almost sixty years old. From my childhood he told me of you two. Of how you came to them through the portal, how you had traveled from 2013, and how you had to return. It's like I've known you my entire life. My father, he died with the machine almost complete. I studied Tesla's diagrams and specifications and completed the portal machine in 1962."

"That's amazing," Elina said. "But why did you bring us back now?"

"I had to. Because of this," Dickie said. He held up an envelope. It was yellowed and looked quite old. Dickie handed it to Elina. She looked at it for a moment. The front of it said "Open on August 13th, 1984."

"What's today?" Tipp asked.

"Today is the 13th day of August, 1984," Dickie said.

She flipped the envelope in her hand and saw that it had been opened. She fished the paper out which had been contained within. She unfolded it and read it.

"Richard Cavalier: Do not waste any time at all. Open the portal now. Use the settings listed below. If you fail, all humanity will be lost forever. The children will help you find the answers in the library. On the book end that contains the game. Tipp will know. Hurry! Do not delay. Yours truly, David Cavalier, September 4th, 1945."

"Who's David?" Tipp asked.

"He was my step brother," Dickie said.

"Was? He's dead?" Elina asked.

"Yes. He died on September 5th, a day after that letter was written," Dickie said. "I don't know why I had to bring you back to 1984, but I know that the world is on the brink of total destruction. The Emperor has all but eradicated humanity. Only small pockets of The Resistance still exist. I've managed to stay here on this island without anyone taking notice. For fifteen years I've lived here by myself. I knew this letter existed. I knew that I had to live until today to find out what it said. I could not risk being killed or for some reason not being able to return here. I have sacrificed most of my life to make sure you two could return safely."

"Wait a second," Elina said. "Where's dad? He was born in 1983."

"Your father was never born, nor was your grandfather," Dickie said. "This 1984, this reality, it's different, it's wrong. You two, you will never be born if this reality continues."

"I don't understand," Elina said.

"I do!" said Tipp excitedly. "When we went back in time, history was changed, right? And because of that, a different reality came into existence, one with the Emperor in charge."

"You've got it so far," Dickie said. "My father said you two were smart, that you would be able to understand."

"So," Elina continued her brother's thought. "The only way to fix things is to go back in time again. To stop the Emperor."

"Correct," Dickie said.

Suddenly the room shuddered. Books fell from the shelves and dust fell from the ceiling. The great chandelier in the middle of the room swayed.

"What was that," Elina asked, fear in her eyes.

"That was the portal machine in the basement self destructing," Dickie said.

CHAPTER 16

It had taken some time for all of the information to sink in for the children. Their great-grandfather spent time explaining the history of the world from 1891 forward.

The yellow-gray creature that had come out of the portal was from another world. No one would ever know all the details of his existence, for the yellow-gray man spoke in riddles and half-truths. After the assault on New York City in 1891, the gray man disappeared, as did his army. The people who fought on that last day of May tried to tell people of the world about what had happened, but no one believed them. Even Dickie's father questioned his memories about the events that had occurred. Had it all just been a dream?

Dickie's father knew he had to continue Tesla's work in secret. He was cautious about who he took into confidence. He didn't trust anyone, and for good reason. The gray man and his army shared a very dangerous skill; they could shape shift.

The yellow-gray man could easily use this skill to spy on Dickie's father. Nikola knew of the skill, and had told Hudson of it. Tesla had seen the little yellow soldier that had been caught in the portal as it closed. Even though only half of it had come through the portal, it was still alive for a few minutes. It tried to shape shift and look like Nikola, but it had died, having been bisected as the portal closed.

With such skills, Tesla knew that the yellow-gray man could move within the population freely. That anything Hudson did could be discovered.

Hudson and Josie escaped the city and managed to make it to the North Country of New York. They purchased the island and began building the mansion. Josie's family who was quite wealthy made funds available to Hudson. Also, Dickie's father made wise use of several patents and many of his investments. The Cavalier family wealth grew enormously.

But, the money and wealth didn't really matter much to Hudson. After that night when the children used the Tesla machine to leap to 1984, Tesla was never heard from again. Hudson was heart broken over it.

It wasn't until 1914 that the Emperor revealed himself to the world, though it was as a man, and not his natural yellow-gray form. He called himself Jefferson Lincoln Washington, though he preferred the initials J.L. He brokered peace between nations and halted a conflict that looked like it would swallow the entire world in war.

He had seemingly come from nowhere. His history was shrouded in mystery, though he said all of the right things, was stunningly handsome, and was naturally charismatic. Not to mention, he was very politically connected. He began as a New York City politician, and worked his way up quickly, becoming a Senator in a very short time. When Archduke Franz Ferdinand was assassinated, it looked as if the world was about to descend into a major, all encompassing world war. J.L. Washington convinced President Woodrow Wilson to send him as a special envoy to Europe to calm the situation.

It worked, and the Nobel Committee awarded J.L. Washington the Peace Prize in 1914. Washington became President of the United States in a landslide vote in 1916. Once he was in power, he slowly broke the entire governmental system from within. He changed his title from President to Emperor and declared the United States, the Imperial Union of Americas. Most people went along with it, since peace and prosperity accompanied his rule.

Apparently for the previous twenty three years, he had positioned his assets, gotten his soldiers elected or put into power by whatever means, all over the world. They all shifted themselves into handsome men who had charisma and charm. The world was a happy place for a few years. Then he started building the machines.

The Emperor had a superior intellect. The technology he created was far more advanced than anything humans had dreamed up yet. It seemed wonderful for a time. He gave people everything they ever wanted.

As Emperor, though, he became power mad. By the 1950's he tried to control the entire globe under his one regime. People resisted, as was their nature. They revolted. He massacred them. For a time, this rule by fear and intimidation kept people controlled, but revolt came again and again. Each time, he killed more and more.

In the beginning, he realized that he could not control humanity with just his soldiers, he needed more. He built machines, robotic killing machines which could keep humanity under control. The machines began as large as tanks, but as more and more were built, they became smaller and smaller. Swarms of robots, the size of house flies, could attack a person and kill them in moments. People no longer dared to rebel. That was when Great Grandpa Dickie moved into the mansion full time.

Dickie knew that the robotic killers would be able to detect the portal machine once it was turned on. It gave off too much energy to go unnoticed. He also knew that if the Emperor got his hands on the machine, then all of humanity would be destroyed. The Emperor would open the portal and let more of his species onto the Earth.

Dickie had to destroy the portal machine.

"But with the machine destroyed, then what are we supposed to do?" Elina asked. "How can we go back and fix it all?"

"I think it's up to you two for the answer now," Dickie said. "The letter said that the book end with the game would hold the answer. What does that mean?"

"How are we supposed to know?" Tipp said.

"Well, look around at all these books. The answer has to be in this library," Dickie said. "So, we will just have to look until we find the answer."

The children looked around the library. The books went from floor to ceiling. A second story contained even more books, only accessible from the spiral staircase and a steel grated walkway which encircled the room.

"But, what does that even mean?" Tipp asked.

"How are we supposed to find it in all these books?" Elina asked.

"I guess we'll just have to start looking," Dickie said.

"What game do you think the letter meant?" Tipp asked.

"The letter said you should know, Tipp," Dickie said.

"What about the baseball games we went to see," Elina offered.

"That could be it," Dickie said.

"Are there any baseball history books?" Tipp asked.

"Several, I think," Dickie said. "You know, for the last fifteen years I didn't venture beyond the island. So, I've read just about all of these books. The sports section is on the second floor, up there." He pointed to a section of shelving atop the spiral staircase.

Tipp didn't move.

"I'll go get them," Elina said. "He's afraid of heights."

She climbed the spiral staircase, located the sports history books and pulled them off the shelf. She brought them back down for the others. There were four books total. Two were on baseball specifically, the other two were on the subject of sports history in general. Each of them took a book and started looking.

"What are we looking for?" Elina asked. "It said book end. It could mean the end of the book, or maybe the cover."

"Right," Dickie agreed. "There aren't any bookends in this library, so it has to mean the books themselves." They turned the books over and over in their hands, looking at the bindings, the back pages, the cover, even the dust jackets.

Tipp continued leafing through the book he had on baseball history. He found the section on the Brooklyn Grooms. It had a listing of each season's win-loss record. In short order he located the 1891 season.

"Does anyone else have anything on the Brooklyn Grooms?" Tipp asked.

The others flipped to their indexes and looked for a listing of Brooklyn Grooms, or Grooms.

"It's not in here," Elina said.

"Nor in mine," Dickie echoed. He looked at the fourth book. "They aren't listed in here either."

"Then this must be the book. It's the only one that has any info on the Grooms in 1891, when we went to the games against the Pirates," Tipp said. He looked and looked, but there wasn't anything. Nothing special that pertained to them or their plight.

"I don't get it," Tipp said finally. "There's nothing here."

"Let me look," Elina said, taking the book from her brother. She looked it over and over, but there wasn't a clue. "There's got to be a hidden message or something. Book end, book end." She repeated.

"David wrote the note. Who's David again?" Tipp asked. "How would he know that I would know what he's talking about?"

"In 1945 I was only twenty-three years old. It was a long time ago. I can try to remember. I was just out of college then. The Emperor still let us go to college then. That stopped in 1950. So, I was here then. I was working on the machine. Trying to create the pieces I needed. My father had died several years before. Mother was living here too. What was I doing in September of 1945?" He asked this of himself. He turned and sat in his high-backed chair. He closed his eyes, trying to remember.

"I give up," Elina said. "I can't find anything." She tossed the book onto the couch. It fell open and almost slipped off to the floor. Tipp reached out and grabbed it. He was about to scold his sister for being so careless when he noticed something.

"It's been so long since I've talked to people," Dickie said, with his eyes still closed. "I think it's shocked my mind. You know, the last person I talked to was an old sailor. He came through in a sail boat. No mechanisms at all. He was sailing by the stars. He stayed for a week. I gave him food."

"I think he's gone mad," Elina whispered to her brother.

Tipp ignored her. He was looking intently at the book. He held it in such a way that the edges of the pages cascaded down, making mini stairs from the front to the back.

"A funny old man. He kept saying that men would rise up again some day and that the machines could not survive without men. That we could just wait them out. They would rust and fall apart but man would survive," Dickie said. "That's what I planned to do. I have medicine here. Food. All I need right here. I even have work. I've stayed busy. My father, he had pages and pages of Tesla's designs. I've made all of them. I've built them all! I built the machine in the basement. The one that brought you here. I built the goggles! Let me show you my work. You'll like the goggles." Dickie leapt from the chair and rushed over to a cabinet. He pulled open the doors and retrieved a wooden box. It was ornately carved with what looked like a battle scene between men and machines. Dickie slid his hands over the box and then opened slowly.

"The goggles," Dickie said. "Tesla's instructions were clear. The key was suspending the gas between the lenses. Once the gas was suspended you could pass the electrical charge through it and it performed perfectly. It wasn't until an energy source was created that was small enough to fit onto the side of the goggles that it could be perfected. The prototype had wires running down to a large backpack of batteries. Completely impractical. Here, try them on."

Elina took the goggles from him and placed them over her head.

"What are they for?" She asked. "They don't seem to do anything."

"I don't know!" Dickie exclaimed. "I don't know what any of the inventions do! I don't know if they work or not. I just built them according to Tesla's specifications as best as possible. He created principles in his instructions, what he was attempting to do, and I tried to improve on his initial designs."

"The briefcase!" Dickie said. "I have to show it to you! When I was to meet you I had to give you the briefcase. But of course it's locked now. I was told to lock it. The briefcase was opened. The combination was set, but I didn't know it. Didn't know it. Didn't know it. Once I was done and I was sure that I was done, I was to put it in and lock it. Put it in and lock it. I will show you." Dickie opened the steel door and ran from the library. "It's for the children! Tipp and Elina get the briefcase!" They could hear him yelling as he ran down the hallway.

"Tipp, he's completely crazy. He's been cooped up in here by himself for decades working on stuff that he doesn't even know if they work or not. He doesn't even know what this stuff is for! Tipp, how are we supposed to get home now? He blew up the machine!" Elina was near tears. Tipp had been ignoring everything around him.

"Look!" Tipp exclaimed finally. He showed his sister what he had found. Along the edge of the book's pages, when the book binding was skewed so the pages cascaded, a picture and writing could be seen. It was a schematic!

"Where's Great Grandpa Dickie?" Tipp asked. "Look what I found!"

Elina looked at the edge of the book and saw what it was. A picture of a metal briefcase was drawn there. Next to it was a series of numbers. Just then their great-grandfather returned.

"Where did you go?" Tipp asked.

"I, uh, just wanted to check something," he said. "What have you got there?" He walked over towards them.

"Tipp found something," Elina said.

"Oh, let's have a look," Dickie said, walking towards them.

"I found it," Dickie said closing the door. It startled the children. The Dickie that was standing next to them froze. The one who had just come in the door had a briefcase in his hand.

"It's one of them!" the real Dickie with the briefcase yelled. "How did it get in here?"

The children shrieked and tried to get away from him. The fake Dickie's skin rippled and it suddenly changed into one of the yellow skinned creatures like in Tesla's lab. It tried to grab at Tipp, but he was too quick. Tipp dodged out of the way and all the creature grabbed was air. Elina wasn't as quick, and she was caught by the collar.

"Leave my sister alone!" Tipp gave a swift kick to the creature's crotch. It gave a pitiful yelp and doubled over in pain, dropping Elina. The two children ran towards the real Dickie. He pushed the children behind him.

"Here, take this," he said to them, handing over the

briefcase. He pushed up his sleeves and started towards the yellow creature. Strapped to his arm was some sort of device. Dickie let out a war cry and leapt into the air. It was an unnaturally high leap. He had devices strapped to his legs as well. It gave him the ability to jump extremely high. He tackled the yellow creature and the two of them rolled across the floor, knocking the high backed chair on its side.

Tipp and Elina ran towards the spiral staircase with the briefcase, but Tipp froze.

"Hurry, Tipp!" Elina cried.

"I can't," he said. "It's too high!"

"We have to! You can do it! I know you can. I've never been more sure of anything in my entire life. Just imagine you're one of your heroes in a video game and you can do it," Elina said.

Tipp started up the stairs. One after the other. His legs felt like rubber. He climbed around and around. He felt like he was going to throw up.

"I can't do it!" he yelled to her.

Below them, their great-grandfather rolled on the floor, locked in combat with the yellow creature.

"You have to!" Elina countered.

Tipp closed his eyes, said a quick prayer for courage, and willed his legs to move. Again, one foot after the other. He pushed himself to climb the spiral staircase.

Finally, Tipp made it to the top. He climbed on his hands and knees over to his sister.

"I don't feel so good," he said.

"Hurry up!" his sister shouted at him.

Tipp looked at the briefcase and saw the combination lock. It was a heavy duty lock with five digits. He rolled the numbers to match the ones that were printed in the schematic they had found on the fore edge of the book. The case popped open.

Inside, fitted neatly into a perfect cutout was, what looked like, a large brass pocket watch, with multi-colored jewels on its case cover. There was a note taped to the mechanism. Elina took out the note and read it.

"It says to open it and hold down both buttons," Elina said. She looked down at her great-grandfather as he was fighting with the yellow creature. They tumbled across the floor. The yellow creature bit Dickie on the arm, and he let out a scream.

"We have to help him," Elina said.

"No, we need to push the buttons," Tipp replied. He grabbed the brass mechanism, opened it and pushed the buttons. It began to buzz loudly. Both the yellow creature and Dickie stopped to look up at the children on the second floor walkway.

The mechanism started to throw the same type of blue-white electricity that the Tesla portal machine had. Suddenly a beam of electricity shot out from the top of the mechanism and formed a portal on the bookshelf.

"Go!" Dickie yelled. The yellow creature swiped at him with its claws and cut him across his chest. Dickie was knocked aside, but he still managed to call to them again. "Go!"

Elina and Tipp hesitated, then ran for the portal. They dove through it. The yellow creature leapt at them, but Dickie shot something from the device on his wrist and the yellow creature was stopped in mid-leap.

The children fell into a pile on the floor. The portal behind them closed, and all was silent. They moved slowly and cautiously, not sure where they had landed. Not even sure what year it was. After a few moments, as their eyes adjusted, they knew exactly where they were.

"We're in the library," Elina said. Her whole body still tingled from using the Tesla machine again. The tingling was uncomfortable to be sure, not to mention the scrapes to her hands and knees from the steel of the catwalk mesh.

"But, it's not the same," Tipp agreed. He grunted through the pain as he got to his feet. The tingle in his lungs made him cough. "Something is different. It's like it's not finished yet."

"It's not," a voice said from the shadows of the room below. "Not yet at least."

Their eyes began to adjust to the dim lights of the library. They went to the railing to see from whom the familiar voice had come.

It was Hudson Cavalier!

CHAPTER 17

Hudson looked to be quite a bit older than he was just a few hours ago when they had left him. He walked with a cane, similarly to how their Great Grandpa Dickie walked in the last few years of his life. The children could hardly contain their excitement. They ran down the spiral staircase and rushed towards Hudson. Tipp had completely forgotten about his issue with heights for the moment.

"I never thought I would see you again," Hudson said. He stooped and opened his arms as the children ran to hug him.

"Amazing," he said. "You look as if you haven't aged a day."

"We haven't," Tipp said.

"It's only been a few hours since we left you," Elina said.

"Amazing," was all Hudson could reply.

"Dad, what's going on?" This came from a young blond haired boy who ran into the room.

"Tipp and Elina, allow me to introduce Richard Cavalier. My son," Hudson said. "And your future great-grandfather."

"Hi," a ten year old Dickie said to the children. "What do you mean, papa?"

"I will tell you all about it, son," Hudson said. "But first, is anyone hungry?"

"I am," Elina said.

"Me, too," agreed Tipp.

"I am, too, papa," Dickie said. He ran towards the kitchen.

Tipp and Elina trailed behind.

"What year do you think this is?" Tipp asked quietly.

"I don't know, but if Dickie is a little boy, then it's not 1984, it must be like the 1930's, right?"

"Yeah," Tipp said. "Why are we whispering?"

"I don't know," Elina replied.

They went into the kitchen for something to eat. It was much different than what Tipp and Elina remembered from their time. The stove was heated by wood, rather than electricity, and there wasn't a refrigerator at all. The counter tops were all hardwood, and there was a hand pump by the sink.

"Whatever you would like, Jacquez can whip it up," Hudson said.

"Where's Josie," Elina asked. Hudson sat down heavily on one of the stools at the counter.

"My dear Josie passed away several years ago. I've since remarried to a wonderful girl named Harriet. She is Richard's mother," Hudson said.

"My half brothers are all grown up and are working with The Resistance near New York City. That's where the Emperor moved the Capital right Papa?" Dickie said.

"Richard, we should not speak of such things unless we are in the library, with the walls that protect our speech from prying ears," Hudson said. "After we eat, we shall all go to the library and discuss matters. I think you children might have some interesting news for us."

"Yes!" Tipp said. "When we left you, we ended up in 1984! And-"

"Tut, tut," Hudson stopped him. "When we are in the library." He looked over a Jacquez who had begun preparing a meal with eggs and bacon."

"What time is it?" Elina asked.

"What year is it?" Tipp added.

"It's August 2nd, 1933," Dickie said.

"And it is approximately seven thirty in the morning," Hudson said, checking his watch and then returning it to his vest pocket, leaving the gold chain to dangle.

"I am all mixed up," Elina said. "Traveling through time makes it confusing."

"You traveled through time?" Dickie asked.

"That's right," Tipp said. "We are bonafide time travelers." He said this with a smile and put his arm around his sister. "Probably the only ones in the entire world."

"No doubt," Hudson said. "And I should think we should try to leave it that way."

"Here you are," Jacquez said with a French accent. "Eggs and bacon, with American hash browns on zee side. Bon appetit!"

"Now then," Hudson said. "Let us enjoy our breakfast. Harriet should be returning from the mainland any moment with new groceries and the supplies for which I sent her."

"She's been gone for three days," Dickie informed them. He was about to dig into his eggs, but Hudson stopped him.

"Dickie! You forget yourself," Hudson said. Dickie bowed his head, and Hudson said a blessing for the meal. After their "amens" the children began to eat as if they were famished.

"I hope you have ketchup," Tipp said.

"But of course!" Jacquez replied, producing a bottle of genuine Heinz brand tomato ketchup.

"Whew!" Tipp was relieved. He covered his eggs and hash browns with ketchup, even as Jacquez said something under his breath in French. He apparently didn't think his cuisine needed the addition of ketchup. Tipp could not disagree more.

They finished their meal, and filed back into the library. Hudson closed the heavy steel door behind them. It was a door that they had first seen in 1984, but hadn't existed in 2013. Of course, things had changed.

Hudson also cranked a wheel by the fireplace, and two large steel doors closed over the tall, floor-to-ceiling windows. The room was now illuminated by electric bulbs in the chandelier, as well as lamps around the room.

"These were not part of the original design," Hudson said, referring to the steel doors. He slapped a hand against them, and they sounded very solid. "However, with the state of affairs of the world being what they are, it provides a level of security to know that no matter what happens out there, the future will be safe in here."

Elina and Tipp looked around the room. The shelving was almost complete, but no books had been moved in yet. The floors were covered with sheets as were the pieces of furniture. It was definitely a work in progress.

"Where are all the books?" Tipp asked.

"They are safe," Hudson said. "They are in storage here on the grounds. I had specially sealed steel crates created and lowered into the cellar through outer access hatches. We had them brought up from New York via a barge. It was quite an operation to smuggle them up here."

"Smuggle?" Elina asked. "You had to smuggle books on a barge?"

"Times are bad, very bad," Hudson said with a great heaviness to his voice. "Our President of these United States secured an alliance with the new Mechanized Army Division and abolished both houses of Congress. He's declared himself Emperor, and martial law has been instituted. He's taken to calling it the Imperial Union of Americas, but I just can't bring myself to call my homeland that. There are still some that believe in the Stars and Stripes, but fewer and fewer. Some of the judges across the country have now sided with him, as have some of the state police. The military has been split, and have been set against each other in battle. Fortunately most of the battles are at sea now, though the mechanized army is limited to land. For five years, war waged in some of the southern states. Most people in the north just accepted their fate.

"Religion was abolished in all its forms. Only homage to the Emperor is allowed. Commerce continues, but there are so many rules and regulations that it makes it impossible to do any kind of business without the Emperor's interference. There are no new inventions, no new ideas, no new innovations," Hudson continued. He walked over to a sheet-covered chair, pulled the cover off and dropped it to the floor. He sat down heavily and put his head in his hands.

"I have to ask you two now," he said finally. "Will you help us?"

Elina and Tipp were quiet for a moment. Everything they were just told seemed too impossible. And yet they had seen, in 1984, how far things would go, how much worse it was going to get. People were going to be all but wiped out on the face of the Earth because of the Emperor. Dickie would be driven to madness. The story of the lone sailor who thought the only answer was to outlast the machines rather than fight them; it told the tale of hopelessness. Now they were being asked to help somehow, as if either one of them could do anything. What could either of them do?

"How? How can the two of us do anything?" Elina

asked. She was nearly crying. It was so terrifying, and there was a thought that was forming in the back of her mind. It was a thought that she was scared to consider. She pushed it away. It wasn't something she was willing to think about now.

"And why us? Why are we so special?" Tipp asked.

"Why you? Because you know that this isn't normal. You know how things were supposed to be. You also know where this goes. You said you came from 1984 after being in 1891? You've seen where things lead. It's not good, is it?"

"No," Elina said. "It's not good." She was looking at Dickie.

"But we're just kids," Tipp argued.

"I know. I know. I wish Tesla were here," Hudson lamented.

"Where is he?" Elina asked. "Can't we go find him?"

"He was taken," Hudson said.

"They took him and locked him up," Dickie chimed in. "He's the only one that would be smart enough to stop the Emperor, so he had to be locked up. We don't even know if he's alive."

"He's still alive," Hudson said. "I have it on good authority that he's alive. The problem is, getting to him. Freeing him. The mechanized army is too powerful, there's no way past."

"Could we use Tesla's portal?" Elina offered.

"It hasn't been completed yet," Hudson said. "I've got the plans, but I haven't built it yet. In fact, how is it that you two managed to make it back without that machine in working order?"

"We used this," Tipp said, handing the small pocket-watch-portal-creating machine to Hudson. "This is what brought us here. We brought the machine with us. There was a note on it that said to push the buttons. But we don't know how to use it to get back. There's a bunch of dials on it."

"Let's have a look," Hudson said. Dickie came up beside him to look as well. Hudson retrieved his glasses from his front vest pocket, and perched them on his nose. He opened the top of the bejeweled portal machine.

Inside were the two buttons which Tipp indicated he had pressed to create the portal. Everything else was confusing. There were dials within dials that had numbers all around them, counting in tens up to ninety. In the center were four additional dials that could rotate up from zero to ten. Hudson studied them intently. He rotated the small mechanism in his hands. Finally he removed his spectacles.

"It's far too advanced for me to make anything of it," Hudson admitted. "I dare say, I would not suggest using it again. It may send you into oblivion."

"That's what we were afraid of," Elina said.

"For now, I fear we must wait to see if my sons are able to free Tesla and organize The Resistance to overthrow the Emperor," Hudson said. His tone revealed that he did not put much hope in it at all.

There was a metallic knock at the library's door. Hudson walked over and slid open a visor that allowed him to view the other side through a thick piece of glass. Satisfied, he slid the visor closed, unlocked the door and spun the great wheel to open it. Jacquez was standing there with a worried expression on his face.

"Sir, a boat approaches at great speed. I saw it through the binoculars. It is coming from the west, sir. A single driver, but someone may be hiding below. He should be here any moment. I fear that it may be someone wishing us harm," Jacquez said. "Perhaps now, you shall trust that I have yours and your family's safety as my greatest concern."

"Perhaps, Jacquez. Perhaps," Hudson said, placing his hand on the man's shoulder. "Retrieve the weapons."

Jacquez ran off as he was commanded. Hudson rubbed his chin with concern. In just a moment Jacquez returned with two rather dangerous looking machine guns that reminded Tipp and Elina of the type used in an old mobster movie. They had the round bullet magazine attachments. Hudson took one from Jacquez and hoisted it confidently. To the children it looked strange that the man they knew as a scientist and inventor would feel so comfortable with a weapon. The world was in a terrible place indeed!

"Children, stay in the library!" Hudson said sternly. Elina, Tipp and Dickie obeyed and closed the heavy steel door upon Hudson and Jacquez' departure, spinning the wheel to lock it fast.

"So, you're from the future," Dickie said. "That's so amazing. There are so many things I want to know!"

"You know what's crazy?" Tipp asked. "You're actually our great grandfather!"

"That's impossible!" Dickie said, sitting down to contemplate that.

"It's true," Elina said. "You get married and you have a son, then he has a son, who is our father. In fact, just before we traveled through time -" she stopped short.

"What?" Dickie asked.

"I don't know if I should say," Elina said quietly. "I mean, I don't know if it's right to tell you. Or if you'll be upset by it."

"I can handle it," he said. "Tell me."

"Just before we traveled through the Tesla machine," Elina said heavily. "You died. You passed away."

Dickie was quiet. He sat on the sheet covered chair, contemplating what that meant, for a long moment. Both Tipp and Elina watched him. They were sad as they remembered the emotions they experienced when they had first been told. It seemed like such a long time ago now. And after all they had been through, it almost seemed like it wasn't even real. Here they were, talking with him. Talking with Dickie when he was just a boy. How was it possible that there was a time when he would no longer exist?

"When did it happen?" Dickie finally asked.

"May 2013," Elina said solemnly. "Our grand parents had gone missing in an expedition near Australia. Our parents had to go search for them. They left us with you in this very house. You were so excited to see us. But then you warned us that you were going to die that weekend."

"Ah ha! So I knew!" Dickie said excitedly. "Do you know what that means?"

"What?" Tipp and Elina asked at the same time.

"It means I knew I was going to die. That we had this conversation. It means that the correct time line includes this very conversation. We're doing the right things. We can make things right!" Dickie said. "Plus, 2013 is a long time from now. It's eighty years! That's a whole lifetime. I've got a long time to go. Don't be sad."

"You know, you never let us go anywhere in the house," Tipp said. "We were never allowed to come into the library."

"I wonder why I wouldn't let you do that," Dickie said, pondering the thought. He looked around the room. "Well, if we had to keep things in place until the right time, until you needed them in your time period then, it would make sense not to ever touch them. To keep it like a time capsule."

"That would make sense," Elina said. "And of course you couldn't tell us that, it would make us more curious about it."

"Absolutely," Dickie said.

"In fact, we already used something out of the time capsule! The book with the writing on the side!" Tipp said.

"You're right. It showed us the combination to find the new Tesla device," Elina replied, she ran her hands through her hair as she did and realized she was still wearing the goggles that 1984 Dickie had given her. "I forgot about these. What do you think they do?"

"I don't know. I thought maybe they were to protect your eyes during time travel," Tipp suggested.

"Then, why weren't there two pairs?"

"Good question," Tipp replied. He was looking around the room now. The shelves had been built, the fireplace was installed. The enormous steel doors that closed over the windows were as solid as could be. From the looks of it, you could drop a bomb on the room and it would still be standing. On the mantle, just above the fireplace was a framed picture.

"Elina, look!" Tipp couldn't quite reach it, but he knew his sister could. She came over, stood on her tippy toes and took down the framed picture.

"That's my father's favorite picture," Dickie said. "His first wife, Josie took it."

"We know," Tipp said. "We were there."

It was the picture of Hudson, Tipp and Elina standing in front of Tesla's machine just before they had headed off for the baseball game. There was something bitter sweet about the picture. Elina still had her computer bag with her, and knew that she had already captured the image herself, but seeing the real thing again almost made her cry. They would never get to see Josie again.

Elina touched the glass and stroked the cheek of Hudson. She wished that Josie had been in the picture.

Just then, there was a knock at the metal door.

"Should we answer it?" Elina asked. She placed the frame back on the mantle.

"Not without checking first," Dickie said. He rushed across the room, pulled a chair over to the door and climbed up to slide open the visor. Climbing down and sliding the chair out of the way, he opened the door.

"David!" Dickie exclaimed.

"Little man!" A tall broad shouldered man walked into the room. He looked very much like Peter, the children's own father. This must have been Dickie's half brother, David Cavalier.

"So," he said to Elina and Tipp. "You must be the time travelers."

They nodded in reply. Hudson and Jacquez entered the room beside David. They both had grave looks on their faces. Hudson walked over to a bar and poured himself a drink of alcohol. He let out a heavy sigh and put his face in his hand. Finally he stood up straight and turned to speak to them.

"Children," Hudson said. "We must leave immediately for New York City. Something terrible has happened. My friend, Nikola Tesla has died."

CHAPTER 18

David Cavalier had arrived by boat. He had raced down stream from Clayton, New York as fast as he could to avoid detection. There was very little in the way of patrols between their island and Clayton. In the other direction, there were plenty of patrol boats and shore outposts. It was dangerous at this time of day. At night it was easier to slip in and out of Alexandria Bay, but in broad daylight he would have surely been spotted. Downstream past Ogdensburg, it was near impossible to traverse the St. Lawrence any longer. The river had been laced with mines and the guns along the shore were now automated. They fired at anything that moved along the water.

Many of The Resistance had found allies in Canadian nationals, as they had managed to avoid having their government become overrun by the Emperor's minions. They weren't much of a military threat to the might of the Imperial Union, but they did prove to be an eventual annoyance.

Canada's military had battled the mechanized army of the Imperial Union with severe losses. The natural boundaries of the bodies of water proved to be an invaluable asset to Canada, however, as water was an extra obstacle for the mechanized army. The Navy and

Air Force of the Imperial Union was locked in battle between each other and seemed to be preoccupied vying for control. With resources directed to those efforts, there wasn't as much effort given to protecting the waterways to the north. People could still escape to Canada if they were careful. The Emperor seemed content to control the territories of the former United States for now. Though everyone understood world domination was his objective, he was held back by the oceans and waterway,at least for the moment. Yet he continued to be frustrated by The Resistance. The odd thing was, a vast majority of humanity was starting to actually side with the Emperor. They were just tired of all the fighting. They were ready to give in.

They all climbed aboard David Cavalier's beautifully polished wooden boat. He started the engine and it roared to life.

"Many people in The Resistance don't like motors, but you have to admit, a Hacker-Craft is a beautiful thing," David said. He slowly backed the boat away from the dock, steered it towards open water and pressed the throttle forward against the stops. It practically jumped out of the water with acceleration. The sun glistened off the spray, and for a moment the children forgot they were racing towards New York to see Tesla before he was buried. It felt like those sunny days when their mother and father would take out the boat for a ride up and down the river. They would dock for lunch at Alexandria Bay and watch the sun go down in Clayton or Cape Vincent . They would sometimes even spend the night under the stars anchored off shore.

As they headed up the St. Lawrence river, they stopped short of entering Lake Ontario and landed at Clayton, New York. They docked and were able to climb aboard the steam train that would take them right into Watertown.

It was the busy part of the year for tourism. Despite the Emperor's reign, people still enjoyed traveling to the Thousand Island region for vacation. They still took the train to the coast. For the Cavaliers, it was a good thing. They blended in well, looking like any other family visiting for leisure rather than traveling on Resistance business.

The trip into Watertown took almost an hour. The depot was by the river, down behind the large and magnificent Woodruff House hotel, which also faced the public square.

The Cavaliers departed and had about two hours before their train would leave for Rome, NY. They took the opportunity to walk through the square.

Tipp and Elina were amazed that many of the buildings looked familiar. The main square in town had many of the same statues and churches which still stood in 2013. They recognized the large clock tower, the Paddock Arcade, the Woolworth Building and the large Empsall Building, all standing in the same locations. Just off the square was the Flower Memorial Library which Dickie had taken them to many times before. It was one of the most beautiful buildings they had ever visited. It looked like it had never changed at all.

A bell rang, and a trolley car rolled past, heading

through the square and down Court Street. The children watched in amazement. They had never known that Watertown was such a busy and bustling town!

Hudson was speaking to Jacquez in private, and then Jacquez walked over to the hardware store on the public square. Hudson decided he was going to try the new restaurant that had been opened by the Dephtereos family. They were calling it the Crystal Restaurant.

They ordered their food, and Tipp was very happy to see both Heinz ketchup and Coca-Cola on the menu. Jacquez joined them shortly, carrying a package wrapped in brown paper under his arm. He leaned and whispered to Hudson, who merely nodded.

The children didn't say anything, but it reminded them of how their parents had been acting during the days leading up to their trip to Great Grandpa Dickie's house. They didn't like it.

They finished their lunch, and paid the tab.

"That was quite good," Hudson said. "I'll have to make sure to come again in the future."

"We know we'll be here in the future," Tipp said to his sister. The Crystal Restaurant was Watertown's oldest established restaurant and was still in business, even in 2013. They had eaten there several times. It really hadn't changed too much over all those decades.

The Cavaliers, along with Jacquez, made their way back to the train depot to catch the afternoon train to Rome, where they would again switch trains and ride into

New York City. As they stood on the platform, Hudson turned to Jacquez.

"Jacquez," Hudson said. "Please make sure Harriet is not frightened by this development. Keep her safe. I fear that the Emperor will be emboldened by Tesla's death and may move against his enemies swiftly."

"You can trust me, Monsieur Cavalier. I swear my allegiance to you and to The Resistance!" Jacquez said with glistening eyes. Hudson took the man by the shoulders, squared him up, and then hugged him.

"I should never have doubted you, Jacquez," Hudson said. "Make sure the package is put in the appropriate location."

"I will," Jacquez replied.

The train pulled into the station, and Elina, Tipp, Dickie, Hudson and David found their way to the first class compartment. Jacquez waved to them as they entered the car, and were shown to their seats by the conductor.

No sooner had they found their seats when the train began to move. On the platform outside the window people waved to their loved ones. Jacquez waved to them. It was nice to have someone to whom they could bid farewell, but it made them miss their parents for some reason. Perhaps it was all the other people, all the other parents and children who were parting ways with tears. Maybe it was just the thought that, like so many others they had met on their adventure, they might never see Jacquez again. Or maybe it was just simply that they missed their parents, and missed them terribly.

"Children," Hudson said. "Perhaps, you should try to get some sleep. I fear that the next few days may be exhausting."

Tipp wanted to watch the countryside go by. He had never taken the train from Watertown, but after just a few minutes, he found himself nodding off. Elina didn't have to be told twice. She was asleep in just moments. Dickie had curled up on his half brother's lap and snuggled in. The three of them had to be roused awake when the train pulled into Rome two and a half hours later.

The five Cavaliers switched trains for another nearly three hour ride to Albany. Once again they were in the first class car, and once again, the children were able to fall asleep. But not until Hudson bought them sandwiches from the food car. The three hour ride stretched to five hours, as there was a delay outside of Schenectady. The Resistance had blocked a section of the track and it needed to be cleared.

It was nearly evening by the time they pulled into Albany. The train they had planned on taking into New York City had left an hour before their arrival. They booked a later train and had about forty-five minutes until it departed. It meant they had plenty of time to get dinner in the Albany station and use the restrooms.

The Resistance was strongest along the Hudson River line. They took advantage of the mechanized army's weakness to water and launched operations from the river. As the rail line ran along the river, it was a vulnerable target, especially under cover of darkness. They could block the tracks or worse. The Resistance knew that they were inhibiting other humans as well as the moving of the mechanized assets, but it was a matter of frustrating the plans of the Emperor. He had many humans who worked for him. They were constantly traveling from Albany to New York. If there was a secondary Capital, Albany was it. Albany had become a huge bustling metropolis unto itself. Schenectady had been one of the foundations for the creation of the electric motor and the growth of mechanization in general. The boom of the Emperor's mechanized creations grew the Albany-Schenectady area into a dual city that had become almost as large as New York City.

This, of course, was news to Elina and Tipp. In 2013 Schenectady and Albany were just starting to come back from nearly a century of economic downturn. According to their father, tech companies were just starting to crop up in the area. He had been investing in some of them.

The Albany train station was busy with people hustling all over, like ants over a busy ant hill. The children saw, for the first time, the mechanized soldiers they had heard about.

The soldiers were about eight feet tall. They had metal plating which was painted flat black and rode on twin tank treads. Where one arm should have been was a large machine gun instead. While the other arm ended with a crude three-fingered hand with an opposable thumb. Their heads could swivel three-hundred-sixty degrees, but had only a single camera lens, so depth perception was limited. The strength of the mechanized soldiers was in their heavy armor and their sheer numbers. Their weaknesses were their poor ability to target and their limitations with uneven or wet terrain. Still, they seemed huge and intimidating.

Within the train station there were about twelve milling about. They would vocalize to the people every now and again:

"Keep moving. Do not dawdle. No loitering. No groups larger than five." The voices were hard and mechanical. To Tipp and Elina it was something out of a sci-fi movie. They were scary.

"Let's get to our platform," David said. He could tell by the looks in their eyes that they were intimidated. Hudson agreed and they all headed towards the platform where their train would be arriving momentarily.

On the platform, another mechanized soldier rolled back and forth. It's head would swivel and scan the people. The treads of the tank-like tracks made a clacking noise on the concrete. The gears of the motor ground heavily and the servos of the head and arms whined as it turned. It was an abomination!

The children clung to Hudson each time it passed them. Finally the train arrived and they all got onto the first class car. It took nearly fifteen minutes for the passengers to climb aboard and for the train to depart towards New York City.

It was eight o'clock at night. As the train left the

bright lights of Albany, the stars and moon could be seen in the sky. For some reason the luminary bodies brought with them a calming effect for Tipp and Elina. They were familiar, like home.

"Those are interesting goggles," David said to Elina. "Mind if I take a look?"

"I forgot I had them," Elina said. She removed them from her head and handed them over to David, who held them up and looked around the cabin of the first class rail car.

"Very interesting indeed," David said. "Where did you get these?"

"Dickie gave them to me. The 1984 Dickie, that is," Elina said.

"Ah," David said. More quietly and closer to Elina, he said, "We should be careful about our conversation. The Emperor has agents all over. They report back whenever they overhear something out of the ordinary. Would you be willing to trade the goggles to me?"

"Sure, for what?"

"Do you like baseball?" David asked sitting upright again.

"It's okay, I guess," Elina said.

"I happen to have a signed, Babe Ruth baseball card," David said.

"That's pretty cool," Elina replied. "Is it worth anything?"

"I'm sure it will be."

"Where is it?"

"It's back at the house on the island. It's hidden in a place that no one will find it. If you trade me the goggles, I'll tell you where it is," David said.

"Okay, deal!" Elina said. They shook on it, and David leaned forward and whispered into Elina's ear. As he whispered, Elina nodded her head in understanding.

"Got it?" David asked.

"Got it!" Elina acknowledged.

"Pleasure doing business with you," David said.

"You too," Elina said.

She turned to Tipp who had been staring out the window watching the scenery fly by in the darkness.

"Hey Tipp, guess what?" she said.

"What?"

"I just traded for a mint condition, signed, Babe Ruth baseball card," she gloated.

"What? No way! Where?" Tipp spun around.

"I don't have it yet, it's back at the mansion," Elina said.

"I don't believe you," Tipp said looking skeptical.

"It's true," she said. David stood and walked over to speak with Hudson.

"Yeah, right," Tipp said to his sister. He turned back to look out the window. "You wouldn't even know what Babe

Ruth was famous for."

"Would, too," Elina said. She folded her arms on her chest and sat heavily back in her chair, frustrated that her plan to gloat over her brother had somehow backfired.

They traveled for another hour or so when they came to the train station in Kingston, New York. It was a normal stop over as passengers departed and more boarded for the remaining leg of the journey into the big city.

"This is new," David said, indicating mechanized soldiers that were boarding. These were smaller versions of the large soldiers the children had seen in the Albany station. They could fit down the aisles of the train and only rose about four feet tall.

"Should we be concerned?" Hudson asked his son.

"I don't think so," David said. "Let's just sit tight and see what happens."

"Do you think news has reached him yet?" Hudson asked.

"Probably. But to mobilize this quickly. I wouldn't think it possible. Nor would I imagine he would think it necessary or prudent. We thought there would be a warning. Perhaps we were wrong," David said.

The mechanized soldiers rolled down the aisles and swiveled their heads to look at each passenger. Most of the passengers paid them no attention. Some tried to hide their faces with newspapers or their hats.

When one of the mechanized soldiers rolled up to the

Cavaliers, the children couldn't help but look. It had much less armor plating that the larger versions, but it seemed more agile and able to get into smaller places. This made it more dangerous. The gun was smaller, but a gun was a gun. The mechanical hand seemed like it had been improved as well. It had five fingers now, including the opposable thumb, and each finger had a rubbery tip.

With a lurch the train started on its way again. The mechanized soldiers would be with them for the rest of the trip into the city. There would be several more stops. More and more people would be getting on. The train was already almost full, and now with the machines in the aisles, it was going to be even more difficult to move within the cars.

The train was well on its way now, and the soldiers continued their survey of the passengers. Just to get up and use the restroom or get to the food car was an inconvenience. You had to wait until the mechanized soldier rolled past.

Most of the passengers tried to ignore it, but some took to grumbling. It seemed that all the grumbling did was attract more attention from the soldiers.

Tipp spent time studying the soldiers as best he could. He was a big fan of sci-fi movies, books, comics and video games. This being 1933, what he saw seemed far too advanced to be fully autonomous and self sufficient. The technology was just too good. It looked more like the type of stuff that was around in the 1980's and 90's. Like the bomb disposal robots. But even those were controlled by somebody. These seemed to be running on their own. Functioning independently.

If this was the result of having the so called Emperor in the world, then it was no wonder things had gotten so bad so quickly. He had used technology that was generations ahead of its time to suppress the population. People simply weren't prepared for it. It wasn't fair!

Maybe that's why Elina and Tipp were so important to The Resistance. They had seen future technology. They could describe weapons of the future, fighting techniques that could be used to combat the mechanized army. Tipp himself had probably destroyed thousands of mechanized robots playing video games all by himself. He was a genius at it! They could train The Resistance and beat the Emperor!

"How much longer," Elina asked. Hudson looked at his watch, leaned across the aisle and showed it to Elina.

"About an hour, dear," he said. He was about to say something else, but the words never left his lips. There was a deafening explosion and the train lurched violently. Hudson was thrown from his seat and tossed down the aisle like a child's doll.

The mechanized soldier in their car went flying forward as did the passengers in their seats. The sound of screeching metal and breaking glass was all around them. The lights went out and their world seemed to go upside down. People screamed, and they were all tossed into the air.

They bounced against seats and the ceiling and each

other for what seemed like an eternity. With each impact came a fireworks display of a million stars, and the sounds became more and more muffled.

And then there was blackness and silence.

It took a few moments for Elina and Tipp to realize that the train had been in an accident. They had ended up entwined with each other in one of the seats. They were relatively unhurt. Just a few bumps and bruises. Dickie was okay too, though he said his ankle hurt. It was dark and difficult to see anything. The train car was at an angle but still relatively upright. The children looked for David and Hudson.

"Children!" It was David. "Are you alright?"

"We're okay," Elina said. She saw that he was holding his arm. "Is your arm -"

"I think it's broken," he said. He also had a cut above his eye that was bleeding. They began looking for Hudson. There were people everywhere. The first class passengers had been mostly older people, the well-to-do. They hadn't survived the accident well. Many of them were dead. Some had bad injuries. They helped who they could, but there wasn't much they could do.

At the end of the aisle, they saw him.

"Papa!" Dickie cried. "Papa!" They rushed towards Hudson. He was laying against one of the seats slumped over on the floor.

He wasn't moving.

David felt his father's wrist, and then his neck. He shook his head. In the moonlight that streamed in through the broken window the children could see that Hudson's eyes were open.

"Dickie, Papa is gone," David said. He took his half brother up in his good arm and hugged him close. Dickie sobbed. Elina and Tipp cried too.

For several minutes they all just cried and cried. Even David sobbed over the loss of his father. Finally he set Dickie down. He found a piece of clothing from one of the suitcases that had broken open in the accident and fashioned a sling for his broken arm. David then reached forward and closed his father's eyes.

He told the children to hold hands and he prayed over his father, asking God to remember him in Paradise. They all said "amen."

"Children," David said quietly. "You need to listen to me. There was a plan in place that when Tesla died, we were to go to New York and I was to rendezvous with my brothers Joseph and Samuel. That plan is still in play. We still need to try to make it to New York tonight."

"But what about Papa," Dickie cried.

"They will put him in a coffin and take care of him," David said. "But we have to try. The Resistance is counting on us. Papa would have wanted this."

"Then," Dickie sniffed. "We need to try. For papa and for The Resistance."

Tipp and Elina nodded in agreement.

They climbed over the cluttered aisle towards the exit and down the train steps to the rocks of the rail bed. As they looked forward they could see the engine of the train was off the rails on its side and on fire. Several of the cars were also off the rails. People were streaming from the train cars, even as wails of despair over the dead could be heard.

"The Resistance must have done this," David said.

"But I thought The Resistance was good," Dickie said to his half brother. The confusion in his voice was unmistakable. "I thought The Resistance were the good guys? I thought we were The Resistance!"

"We are. Every war kills innocent people," David said with seriousness. "All wars are bad. All people who bring war have the blood of innocent people on their hands, whether they wish it or not."

Suddenly there was the echo of gunfire. Screams erupted from the crowd. The ricochet of bullets striking the metal of the train cars was unmistakable. Someone was firing at the survivors!

"Quickly! To the water!" David cried. The children ran down the bank towards the Hudson River. They splashed into it waist deep and then ducked low so just their heads were above the surface. Elina held her bag above her head so her tablet computer wouldn't get wet. Tipp held the Tesla machine high above the water as well. They waded into the tall grass and driftwood, which allowed them to be out of the water a bit more and crouch low so as not to be seen. They turned to see the mechanized soldiers shooting at the people who were coming off the train cars.

"Children," David said. "Don't look. Come close. Don't look at it." He held them close to him, shielding them from the sight. It was clear what was happening. The order had come down. If The Resistance wanted to cause a train wreck, the Emperor was going to give them a train wreck, complete with a fresh slaughter of survivors. News writers and cameramen would be along at daybreak to record the massacre.

Just then spotlights came on from the water. Boats with soldiers of The Resistance! It drew away the attention of the mechanized soldiers. The people from the train scattered under the rail cars, even as the machines advanced towards the water's edge. The Resistance soldiers fired on the mechanized soldiers, blasting them to pieces. The gun fire was deafening. The children held their hands over their ears and closed their eyes. It was all so terrible. Explosions of fire, blasts of orange and white lighting the night sky. The heat and concussion was so close it felt like they were going to be consumed by it. Finally, just as quickly as it had started, the gunfire stopped. The mechanized soldiers were destroyed. All was quiet. The spotlights on the boats were dimmed. Voices of men on the boats could be heard as they called to one another, coordinating their next moves.

"The night is darkest before the dawn!" David called out to them. They went silent. There was no reply for a moment.

"But the hope of a new dawn is always bright!" an answer finally came.

"And day break shall come!" David said.

"Brother!" A spotlight shown onto them.

"We need to get to the city," David said.

"We'll get ya there," the voice said. "Help 'em aboard."

CHAPTER 19

Dickie was quiet as the boat traveled down the Hudson River towards New York City. The men on the boat had given them all blankets so that they might try to dry themselves, but it was no use. They were still damp and cold. Elina and Tipp huddled together, shivering. David put his good arm around Dickie.

David spoke to the men of The Resistance about their progress. They apologized about Hudson's death. They seemed very sorry about it. Each of them claimed to have lost someone they loved because of the battle against the Emperor. It didn't make any of the children feel better at all. What they had witnessed had been horrible. The machines killing the people, the train wreck, the death and destruction. It was all a nightmare.

The thought that Elina had pushed away before, now came flooding back into her mind and she couldn't keep it away. She couldn't control her emotions and she began to weep. She cried uncontrollably.

It was their fault! Her's and Tipp's. If they hadn't turned on the machine in their great-grandfather's basement none of it would have happened at all. If they had just left it alone they wouldn't have gone back in time and then the monsters wouldn't have been able to come through and then none of this would have happened and Hudson wouldn't have been killed and Dickie wouldn't go mad in 1984. It was all their fault. The world was being destroyed because she and Tipp had flipped a switch.

She cried and cried. Tipp tried to make her feel better. He thought that she was just scared or felt bad because of what had happened to Hudson. He didn't know what she was thinking. But he just kept patting her on the back and telling her it was going to be okay. That they were going to be fine and were going to make it home.

Elina didn't know how they were going to make it home now. Hudson was dead. Tesla was dead, and they didn't know how to use the time machine. Any future they went to would be ruled by the Emperor. Maybe there was no way to stop it. Maybe it was inevitable.

Great Grandpa Dickie had known it was going to happen before he had died in 2013. The picture had already existed. The note had already existed. The machine was already there. There was no way to stop it. And now Tesla and Hudson were both dead. If there was one man who could have figured out how to have put it all back the way it was, it was Tesla. There was no hope. And yet, they were still going to New York. Why?

She looked at her brother who was shivering next to her, trying to be strong for her. He looked so much older now than when they had started their adventure. She trusted him more now. They were a team. They had been through so much. She squeezed him tighter and gave him a kiss on the cheek. He looked at her as if to say he understood what she was thinking, and he agreed. They would keep going to see what happened, and no matter what, they would go together, stay together and come back together, just like Dad had always told them.

The ride down the river took nearly two hours. They were let off under the George Washington Bridge. At least that's what the children knew it as. The Emperor had probably renamed it after himself. David said goodbye to The Resistance members, and the boat turned back north on the Hudson River.

"I have some friends that we can connect with not too far from here," David said. "Just a few minutes' walk. Do you think you can manage?"

The children all acknowledged that they could, and followed David up the bank and onto the street. They walked through Harlem for several blocks to 177th Street. There they entered an apartment building and went up to the second floor. David knocked twice quickly, paused, knocked once, paused again, then two more times. The door opened and a black man welcomed them in.

"David," the man said. "So good to see you. Are you okay?"

"Isaiah," David said, hugging the man. "No, I'm not. Things are bad. My father was killed on the way down. We've received word that our worst fears have been realized. Tesla is dead. We're trying to make it down to arrange for his funeral. They were to release his body to my father. Now I don't know what will happen."

"Who are these children then," Isaiah asked.

"Isaiah Conklin, this is my half brother Richard, we call him Dickie, and two very interesting people, Tipp and Elina. They are time travelers from the year 2013. They used Tesla's invention to travel here. I'm hoping they can help us put things right," David said. There was a sudden recognition for the children.

"Conklin?" Elina asked. "Our dad is best friends with a man named Conklin in our time. He looks just like you! He's with the FBI."

"The what?" Isaiah asked, as he shook Tipp's then Elina's hand.

"The Federal Bureau of Investigation. It's like the Federal Police," Tipp said.

"Well, maybe he's a relative," Isaiah said. "Police work does run in the family."

"Isaiah is a detective here in New York. Even though he works on the police force, he's part of The Resistance," David informed them.

"It helps to have a man on the inside," Isaiah said. "I'd introduce you to my children, but I'm afraid they've all gone to bed. Maybe I can get you some dry clothes and you can get some sleep yourselves."

"That would be good," David said. "We have to get downtown first thing in the morning. I will be meeting my brothers. They don't know that father has died yet."

"Okay. Let's get the children down and then you and

I can discuss a few things," Isaiah said. Dickie, Tipp and Elina changed into some of the clothes borrowed from Isaiah's children. Dickie still hadn't said a word.

They curled up with blankets on the living room floor and fell fast asleep. The voices from the kitchen didn't keep them up at all. Nor did they stir when the phone rang at 2am. When David's brothers arrived an hour later, the children were still sleeping. It wasn't until six in the morning, when David woke them, that they realized that David's brothers, Samuel and Joseph had arrived.

David was the oldest. He was thirty-two. Samuel was twenty-nine. Joseph was twenty-seven. He had been named after his mother Josephine. She had died when he was thirteen. Hudson had remarried when Joseph was fifteen and away at school. Dickie had been born two years later. Samuel and Joseph took turns giving their little half brother a hug. They also gave Elina and Tipp a hug as well.

"We are honored to meet both of you," Samuel said on behalf of his younger brother. "We must hurry, but Isaiah and his wife have kindly prepared breakfast for us all."

True enough, Isaiah's wife Sarah had made a huge breakfast of eggs, bacon, sausage, fried potatoes, orange juice, coffee, milk and biscuits. Her three children, Isaiah Jr., Michael, and Olivia were all awake now, and were about the same ages as Dickie, Tipp and Elina. As the children chattered away, the adults talked about the train wreck, The Resistance, and the news about the western front.

Apparently, Colorado had successfully destroyed the Emperor's forces there, and were pushing across Kansas towards Kansas City. It was the biggest news of The Resistance movement in nearly a decade.

David showed his brothers the goggles that he'd traded from Elina. Each of them tried them on and talked about them with a level of excitement. Isaiah discussed the new mechanized soldiers that David and the children had seen on the train and how they were being used now within the housing tenements in the city. Before the Emperor had always needed to rely on humans to go into buildings. He was now creating more and more mechanized soldiers to take the place of humans. Soon, he would no longer need humans at all.

After they had eaten to their full, they said their goodbyes. David, Samuel, Joseph, Dickie, Elina and Tipp all left for midtown, where they would attempt to retrieve Nikola Tesla's remains.

In the morning light, the city had started to resemble the one that Tipp and Elina knew. It had grown up quite a bit since they were last here in 1891. The Empire State Building now stood high above the other buildings. The Chrysler Building, with its glistening spire, also stood proudly in the skyline. Of course the rest of the buildings had yet to catch up, but there was a level of familiarity for Tipp and Elina that had been missing before.

"First," David said. "We are going to the city morgue. That's where Tesla's body is. He had been in a secret prison here within the city for the last twenty or so years.

The Emperor made sure that no one was able to get to him. Even Isaiah couldn't pin down his whereabouts. Two days ago, we received word that he had passed away. Fortunately, we have a man in the morgue. For some reason Tesla's body was transported there. It was the first time we had verified his location in nearly five years. I guess if there's one thing we can count on in the Emperor's government it's following the procedure manual. Our man was instructed to cremate the remains, but he substituted another body at our request and placed Tesla's remains in a secure location."

"There's a plan that has been put in place," Samuel said. "We all have a part to play."

"You two were the final piece of the puzzle," Joseph said, holding up the goggles that Elina had traded to David.

"Us?" Elina asked.

"You shall see," David said.

The city morgue was located downtown. To get there, they took the subway system. It was loud and hot. The summer heat, even at this hour of the morning, was unbearable. To Elina and Tipp it made them wonder about global warming. The temperatures didn't seem much different than in 2013.

After nearly an hour, the group came to the subway station they wanted. The morgue was near City Hall, so they got off at City Hall station and ascended through the magnificent architecture. Elina and Tipp had never been to this station stop before. It was amazing with its arching tiles and grand chandeliers. There were bronze statues of men and women who were posed to look as if they were walking about.

Once they made it to street level, it was only a short walk to the building that housed the morgue. The morgue was a quiet, dimly lit, basement section of the hospital. The walls were a dull, mint green that Tipp hated. It was the worst color in the world as far as he was concerned.

The three older brothers entered into the back area, while making the children wait for them in chairs in the hallway. The children did not mind at all. None of them wanted to see a dead body, even if it was their friend Tesla. Dickie had never met Tesla. He was born in Watertown and since he had been born they had always lived on the island, building more and more of the mansion. Tipp tried not to let the depressing color of the paint get to him, but it wasn't easy.

"I miss Papa," Dickie said to Elina and Tipp.

"I know," Elina said. "I'm sorry."

"Is that how he was supposed to die," Dickie asked. "I mean, did I tell you about how he died?"

"You never talked about it," Elina said, somberness in her voice. "At least not that I can remember."

"I don't remember you ever talking about it, either," Tipp said.

"Oh," Dickie said quietly. "I think that if it was important, I would have mentioned it."

"What do you mean," Tipp asked.

"I just mean, time right now, for you two, is overlapping. In the future, I can share with you information that you could benefit from now. Does that make sense? If I'm careful, if I remember as much as possible, I could help you make the right decisions, I could protect you. I could save you. Maybe I could save Papa. Then again, if I could have saved Papa, I would have already. Maybe, there was no way to save him," Dickie said.

"Maybe, in order to save him, this has to happen, and then, none of this will happen," Tipp said.

"Like something will have to happen before this to change everything?" Dickie asked. "Well it might be after this for you two, but it would be before this for everybody else."

"Maybe," Tipp suggested.

"Maybe, you're right," Dickie said.

"I don't know what you two are talking about," Elina said.

Just then, Samuel, Joseph and David came through the double doors from the morgue. They had smiles on their faces, which seemed strange for having just seen Tesla's dead body.

"Why are you three smiling?" Elina asked.

"Because, my dear Elina," David said. "We are going to have the biggest, most grand funeral this city has ever seen!"

CHAPTER 20

The New York Times carried the story of the train accident on the Hudson River line. There was no mention of The Resistance, but rather, of a non-union defect in the rails that had been used. The rail line had assured the public that it would no longer use any non-union supplies. There was no mention of any passengers being shot, nor any mention of mechanized soldiers being blown to pieces, or their rounds being found embedded in the side of the rail cars.

The paper also carried an obituary that announced the death and funeral arrangements for Nikola Tesla. It was carried in the evening edition, the more popular of the two editions of the paper. Most of the city was now informed of a funeral that was never meant to take place, according to the will of the Emperor. Most people would not appreciate the level of rebellion the funeral represented. Tesla was meant to be an unperson, a forgotten entity. He was locked away, never to be heard from again. His death was to be handled quietly, his cremation, done in secret. The fact that there was to be a public viewing and funeral was a direct affront to the Emperor. But, now that it was public news, there was not much that could be done. The public knew nothing about Tesla's ties to the Emperor or the Emperor's true origins. To make any type of public fuss over the funeral, would only invite further inspection and curiosity. All that the Emperor and his people could do was let it proceed and punish the perpetrators after the fact.

The location of the funeral home was chosen by the Cavalier boys with care. The owner was a loyal member of The Resistance and could control who came and went. The only door that was unlocked was the front, and Resistance members were stationed there with concealed weapons. There were also Resistance security forces across the street and at both ends of the block. There would be ample warning if the Emperor decided to make an all out assault on the proceedings.

The funeral home was something of an anomaly. The basement linked in with an underground tunnel system which connected six of the buildings on that block. The buildings used to belong to the same owner and the tunnels were used by the workers during the winter months so they wouldn't have to deal with the cold outside when moving from building to building. If there were to be any type of attack, the Cavaliers could escape through the tunnels.

As Samuel, Joseph, David, Dickie, Elina and Tipp entered the funeral home, the men with concealed weapons nodded knowingly to them. They were large men, and their demeanor was unmistakable. They were there to make sure no one from the Emperor's side tried to disrupt the solemn occasion, whether they were mechanized soldiers or otherwise.

The large room was quiet. Chairs were setup, but there wasn't going to be any type of memorial service, just a public viewing of the great inventor. The six members of the Cavalier family approached the casket.

Tesla looked so life-like. He didn't look dead at all. The funeral director had done an excellent job with the makeup. Even his hands, which were crossed gracefully on his chest, had color to them. He did look much older than the children had remembered. His cheeks were sunken and his hair had lost the deep dark luster of his youth.

Before anyone else was allowed in, the family took their positions. Heavy curtains were drawn closed behind the casket, and large wreathes of flowers were positioned in front of the curtains. In front of the casket, another set of tasseled curtains were held open by beautifully gilded ropes. Flowers were in large ceramic vases on the floor in front of those curtains. The casket itself was up on a stage of sorts. It was a step up from the main floor.

Three chairs had been arranged on the stage for the three children, while David and Samuel took positions by the opened curtains, ready to welcome and greet those who had come to pay their respects. Joseph announced that he had documents to attend to with the funeral home and went behind the curtains behind the casket. Apparently those curtains closed off another section of the funeral home.

At precisely two o'clock in the afternoon, the front doors were opened, and those who wished, were allowed in. There was a steady stream of well wishers. The children didn't recognize any of them. They looked like college professors and scientists. Most were all older, with white or gray hair. They were the only ones left who remembered who Tesla was.

At around three, Isaiah Conklin and his wife came in, shaking the hands of David and Samuel and saying hello to the children. They paid their respects to Tesla and then left quietly. Both Elina and Tipp wished that the Conklins lived in 2013 so they could be friends with their children. They were nice people.

Even though they had been sitting through the whole thing, the children were growing tired. They began to fidget in their seats. The clothes they had been lent by the Conklins, dress clothes, were a bit tight and uncomfortable.

"When is this supposed to end?" Tipp asked, quietly.

"I'm not sure," Dickie said.

"Me, either," Elina whispered.

The stream of people coming in to pay their respects had all but stopped. A lone person every now and then would walk in, shake hands, look at the body, then leave. It had been about ten minutes since the last visitor when a very elderly gentleman came through the door. He walked with a cane. He was tall once upon a time, but old age had bent him over, and made him much shorter now. He was dressed in a fine suit and hat, and sported a long gray mustache.

It seemed to take him forever to walk to the front of the room. He stopped and spoke to David in hushed tones.

He shook David's hand, concern and sorrow in his eyes. He walked over and shook Samuel's hand and nodded as Samuel said a few things to him. Next he walked towards the casket. The step up onto the stage was strained, but with the assistance of the cane, he made it. He walked over to the casket and placed both of his hands on the edge. He removed his glasses and leaned in for a closer look.

For some reason, this whole scene had captivated the children. Perhaps because there was nothing else going on at the moment, or perhaps because there was something not quite right about the scene. Something rehearsed, something peculiar, something just a bit off.

From behind the curtain, where Joseph had gone to "attend to documents" came a distinct clearing of a throat. David and Samuel immediately unhooked the golden ropes that were holding open the curtains in front of the casket and pulled the curtains closed.

And then Nikola Tesla sat up.

"Good day, Emperor," Tesla said. "Checkmate."

He threw a switch from within the casket and a bolt of electricity shot through the side of the casket up through the Emperor's hands and down into the stage. The Emperor went stiff and rigged with a convulsion from the energy coursing through his body. The facade of the old man that the creature had been masquerading in, slipped away. The yellowish features, the large eyes, became apparent. The creature's jagged teeth bared in a howl of pain as the electricity contracted all of its muscles at once. Tesla flipped the switch again, shutting off the power. The Emperor crumpled to the floor, unconscious. Wisps of smoke rose from the Emperor's clothing where they had been singed from the bursts of electrical energy.

Joseph rushed from behind the curtain, the goggles on his face.

"It worked!" He said.

"Of course it worked," Tesla said, vaulting out of the casket. The Cavalier brothers grabbed the creature who had anointed himself as the Emperor and hoisted him up into the casket. They closed the cover, and quickly wheeled it down the ramp and out the back. The children raced after them, barely aware of what they had just witnessed.

A horse drawn hearse was waiting for them, driven, of course, by a member of The Resistance. Tesla and the Cavaliers all climbed into the back of the hearse and the driver coaxed the horses into a trot.

"What just happened?" Elina asked in amazement.

"Why we just played a gambit, a con, on the corrupt leader of this Imperial Union of Americas," Tesla said. "We have set us free!"

"Thanks to you two, and your goggles," Joseph said.

"I don't understand," Tipp said.

"The Emperor and his minions could disguise themselves, they could shape shift. These goggles allowed us to decode the visual frequency by which they tricked our eyes. The goggles created a halo around anyone who was shape shifting, as shape shifting vibrates the air, ever so slightly. Tesla had smuggled the plans out. We had placed the plans in the library on the island. Sometime in the future, Dickie here built them. You brought them back. It all makes perfect sense," David said.

"Maybe to somebody, but not to me," Elina said.

"But you were dead!" Tipp said.

"Ah, that was the dangerous part," Tesla said. "How to fake my death? Of course we had to wait for you children to arrive. Once I received news of your arrival, I simply informed my guard that I wasn't feeling well. They took me to the infirmary. I was hooked to the machines. Machines are easy to fool these days. People who work for the Emperor are taught to listen to the machines, not to think. When the machines said I was dead, I was dead. The danger came in making sure the fools didn't incinerate me before our man intercepted my very much alive body!"

"How did you receive the news that we had arrived?" Elina asked.

"The machines told me," Tesla said. "They send their messages through the air. The energy signature given off by an open portal was recorded in the Watertown area and that information was transmitted to New York City. I've been waiting for that specific information for years. When it came through the ether, I knew you had arrived."

"You hacked their system," Tipp said. "Awesome!"

"I intercepted their transmissions and used it against

them," Tesla replied.

"What happens now?" Elina asked.

"Now we get this retched, imperialistic, self appointed, god-emperor into a secluded prison and throw away the key, get you two back to your own time, and try to put back in place the broken pieces of our society," Tesla said.

"Just like that?" Elina asked.

"Just like that," Tesla said.

"It's over then?" Tipp asked.

"Yes, son. It's over," Tesla said.

CHAPTER 21

Samuel and Joseph left with the Emperor in the casket, heading to an undisclosed prison. They had taken the time to bind his wrists and ankles with steel chains and locks. They also fastened a steel collar around his neck which chained to his wrists and ankles. These they chained to loops within the casket. Apparently the casket had been specially designed for this specific task. It was a steel cage underneath a wooden veneer. Several holes were punched through to give the vanquished Emperor ample air, though no one would have been too broken up if he suffocated in there. Once he was secured in place, the casket was closed and the lid was also padlocked. They were taking no chances.

Tesla, David and the children headed to Penn Station. For Tipp and Elina, this was where their adventure had begun. It seemed like it was an eternity ago, and yet, according to the calendar, it wouldn't happen for another eighty years. They missed their parents, and now with Tesla alive, their chances of reuniting with them seemed brighter than ever. But even as hope and happiness had entered their lives, the realities of Dickie's life and the loss of his father weighed upon them.

A crate, which carried the body of Hudson Cavalier,

was waiting for them at Penn Station. It had been loaded onto a train at the accident site and brought into the city. Hudson had carried identification, and Harriet had been informed by telegram, as they did not have a phone on the island. She sent another telegram to hold the body there at the station for her sons, as they would surely be along to claim it.

David and Dickie would take their father back to the island and, along with Harriet, bury him there. Despite its success, the plan had not been without its losses.

On the train ride back to Albany, Tipp allowed Tesla to inspect the hand held time travel device. For nearly twenty minutes Tesla turned it over in his hands, studying the details. Focusing on a single dial for what seemed like minutes on end.

"It's just as I envisioned it," Tesla said. "Whoever the craftsmen was, he was very precise. You used it to travel here?"

"Yes. We pressed both buttons," Tipp said.

"It created a portal that you then were able to pass through. The portal, after a short amount of time closed behind you, correct?" Tesla asked.

"That's right," Tipp said.

"Just as I envisioned," Tesla said. "My calculations were accurate. I knew they would be. You see, it is not so much time travel, as it is unifying the waves, the frequencies that make up the waves that are time and space. Or more accurately bringing those waves into congruity for a brief moment. What I first understood to be energy or electricity is actually much greater than that. Much more, indeed. It's actually the very fabric which holds all things together. Gravity, energy, mass, time, light, everything, it's all derived from the same dynamic. Once you can capture the correct frequency, you can control it. And once you understand how to control it, one will find it takes very little energy to manipulate it. You can hold it in the very palm of your hand." For emphasis he held up the brass time travel machine.

"But isn't it a dangerous power to have?" Elina asked. "If that fell into the wrong hands, it could be used for evil."

"Of course, child, you're right. The person who possessed this would be much more than human, he would be a god. He would no longer be bound by the laws of life and death. He could travel where ever and whenever he wished. It would be a very seductive and tempting power to use," Tesla said.

"Then, it should be destroyed," Tipp said.

"But, also, think of the good that could be gained from it," Tesla said. "Imagine, all of the wars that could be prevented. Imagine, all of the plagues that could be stopped. The technology that could be brought back to those who never had it. The advancements that could be made. Why, the possibilities are endless."

"The dangers are endless as well," David said.

"Could you go back and save Papa?" Dickie asked. All

of them fell silent. It was a very important question that was at the very crux of such a device. Should it be used to go back in time and keep someone from being killed like Hudson had been.

"If I did that," Tesla said quietly. "Dear Richard. If I did that, then there is the chance that the Emperor may not have been captured. The risk of destroying that is too great. I'm sorry. I mourn the loss of my dear friend Hudson as well."

Tears welled up in Dickie's eyes even as Tesla finished telling him this. He buried his head in David's chest, and David curled his good arm around the boy. Tipp and Elina weren't sure if that was a good excuse or not.

"Why couldn't you just go back in time and stop yourself from making the time machine in the first place?" Tipp asked. "That would stop the creature from coming through the portal, and then none of this would have ever happened, right?"

"That's true, but then whomever went back would be stuck there, as the entire history after that point would never exist, and therefore a time machine would never be built and therefore they would not be able to return. In fact, there's a good chance that they would cease to exist the very moment they stopped the machine from being built," Tesla said.

"So, it would be a suicide mission," Elina said.

"That's right," Tesla said.

The train stopped at the Kingston station, but no

mechanized soldiers came on. Several were on the platform, but they weren't moving. No one seemed to notice them. Within several minutes, the train was moving again, heading towards Albany.

David took the children to the food car and purchased dinner for them. Tesla claimed he wasn't hungry, so he stayed at their seats in first class. They didn't just have snacks, they had a genuine meal. Steak, potatoes, string beans, and Coca-Cola! Of course Tipp asked for ketchup and was presented with a bottle of Heinz brand, much to his pleasure. They took their time and enjoyed every bite. Even Dickie, who's heart was heavy with the loss of his father, found the meal to be pleasing.

When they returned to their seats, Tesla was staring out the window as the scenery flew by. They passed several crossings, where automobiles were lined up waiting for the train to pass.

"Now that the Emperor has been over thrown, do you think that people will start driving cars more?" Tipp asked.

"Perhaps," said David. "It will take some time, though. I'm sure if it wasn't for the mechanized soldiers people would have switched to cars much more quickly by now."

"You know," said Tesla. "While I was imprisoned, I devised an automobile that ran on nothing but electricity. It grabbed the electricity from the ether and converted it for use in a small electrical engine. It could run for hundreds of miles. No one would be interested in it because it would be too quiet. People would claim it to be devilry." He laughed as he said it.

"Wow," Tipp said. "We could use that in 2013."

"Perhaps I will inscribe the designs for you, and you can craft it," Tesla said. He reached over and tussled Tipp's hair. "If they aren't afraid of your computer tablet, then they surely will accept a bedeviled automobile."

They fell silent for the rest of the ride into Albany. Before they reached the station, David went to find a conductor to make sure his father's coffin was properly removed from the baggage car and switched over to the train bound for Rome. They would have to do the same thing in Rome for the train heading up to Watertown.

Tesla took the children to the Rome train, and when they found their seats in first class, they fell fast asleep. They didn't even stir when David came in to sit beside them. The train was halted and inspected in Schenectady, as there was suspicion of Resistance members aboard. The inspectors didn't bother Tesla or David, as they assumed they were no trouble, what with the sleeping children and all.

By the time they arrived in Rome, it was nearly ten o'clock at night. There was a final 10:15 train leaving for Watertown, and they had to practically run to catch it. David had to pay a steward twenty dollars to run with his father's coffin on a push dolly to make it to the other train on time.

The children, still tired and out of breath, flopped into their seats and resumed their slumber. David tried to stay awake, but he too eventually gave in and closed his eyes. Tesla did not fall asleep. His eyes remained open.

He reviewed the conversations of the day in his mind. He made calculations, he devised new devices, he plotted alternative solutions to perceived problems. His brain continued to work.

Once they reached Watertown, it was well after midnight. Rather than make the two hour trip to the mansion, David paid for several rooms at the spectacular Woodruff House hotel in downtown Watertown, right on the square. Hudson's coffin was stored in the basement freezer, and they were all able to have a nice night's sleep.

The morning came very quickly, and for Elina and Tipp, it was very disorienting. It had been awhile since they had slept in a nice hotel bed. When they awoke, it was as if the previous week had been a bad dream. It took a few moments for them to realize that they were still in 1933. The fixtures in the bathroom were the giveaway. Each of them took turns in the hot shower, and by eight o'clock there was a knock at their door. David was ready to take them down for breakfast.

They ate their morning breakfast in the hotel's restaurant as David and Tesla read *The Watertown Daily Times*. The front page story was about the Emperor's disappearance and how a new form of government was immediately being formed that followed the original United States Constitution. A President would be sworn into office by the end of the week and a general election would be held in six months. Additionally, mechanized soldiers would be disassembled and outlawed. People were smiling and chattering at all the tables around them.

There was a general sense of joy and relief. Even Dickie was smiling this morning.

When they had finished their breakfast, they headed down to the train depot to take the steam train out to Clayton. It took nearly an hour to reach the small lake front town of Clayton. The bright sunlight wasn't enough to brighten their moods. For the most part, they rode in silence, watching the countryside drift by. Arriving in Clayton, David arranged for assistance to get Hudson's casket loaded into his boat so they could be on their way. Four men aided in the task. All four refused payment. Once the boat was loaded, they shoved off for Cavalier Island.

It was another thirty minutes through somewhat choppy water before they arrived at the dock of the island. Harriet and Jacquez came down from the house to meet them. It was clear that Harriet had already come to grips with the dreadful news. She had on her brave face for her young son. Dickie was out of the boat and up the dock before they had even tied off. He hugged his mother and she hugged him. She tried to stay strong, but she broke down and both of them cried and sobbed. It was difficult to watch, even for David and Tesla. Once the boat was secured, David walked over to Harriet and gave her a hug.

"Thank you for bringing my son home safely," she said to David.

"I'm sorry we lost father," David said. "But if you heard the news, he did not die in vain. His death has brought about revolution. His death has brought down a titan. The

Emperor has fallen. This will be his legacy throughout the history of the Cavaliers."

"I know it will be," Harriet said through tears. "Children, come with me up to the house. The men will tend to Papa."

The children all followed obediently as Jacquez, Nikola and David moved the coffin onto a cart on the dock. They solemnly wheeled the cart up to the house. A grave would be dug out behind the house. There was a meadow there, that would allow them to dig six feet down and place a headstone. Hudson would forever be entombed on the island.

Inside the house, Harriet poured lemonade for the children and fixed snacks for them. She was happy to have Dickie home and safe, even as she was grieved to have lost her husband. As he told her about their adventure, her eyes lit up and she hung on his every word. It reminded Elina and Tipp of their own mother.

"It's still an hour or so before lunch," Harriet told them. "Why don't you go outside and play for awhile. I will fix lunch and call you when it's ready."

The children didn't have to be told twice. They ran out the front door. For the first time in a long time they felt free. If they had to think about it, the last time they felt this kind of freedom was back before they had been forced to pack the taxi cab and head up here because their grandparents had gone missing. From that point on, Elina and Tipp had found themselves in one problem after another. Now they were running through the woods, free as the wind, laughing and giggling.

Dickie decided a good game of tag was in order, and he tagged Elina. Both Tipp and Dickie proved to be faster than Elina, but she was more determined. She tracked down her younger brother, and they fell to the ground out of breath. He regained his breath and then set off after Dickie. Because, of course, there were no tag-backs. Tipp was able to match his speed straight out, but Dickie was shifty and quick, dodging right or left just as he was about to be tagged. Tipp kept after him and just as they broke into a clearing, Tipp tagged him.

Tipp, completely winded called time out. This was fine with both Elina and Dickie, as they too were out of breath. So much so that Elina's side was hurting. After a few moments of rest, they looked around.

"Hey, I know this place," Tipp said.

"Yeah, me too," Elina said.

"Really," Dickie asked. "How?"

"In the future, in 2013, you brought us, or I guess, you bring us here. You show us a door. It's right here," Tipp said. He showed on the rocks where the door was and then pointed to where the key pad was. "Then you made us promise to remember the number. The code. You said it might some day save our lives."

"Really?" Dickie asked. "Wow, I guess I have a lot of work to do."

"You know, I keep wondering," Elina said. "Why us? I mean, why Tipp and me?"

"I don't know," Dickie said. "Why any of us?"

"Maybe, it's this island," Tipp offered.

"Maybe, it's because my father was friends with Tesla," Dickie said. "Nikola never had children of his own. Papa told me. So maybe that's why. Maybe our family is tied to him, a strange kind of connection."

"Maybe," Elina said.

"Or, it could just be an accident," Tipp said. "It might just seem like it's on purpose because of the way time overlaps, but, it's really just accidental. Maybe, that's how things work all the time. Like, maybe, time overlaps in different ways and that's why it seems like things happen for a reason. But, it's really just an accidental time overlap."

"Interesting," Dickie said.

"Okay, I can't take this kind of chatter any more," Elina said. "You're it!" She tagged Tipp and ran back towards the house.

"Wait! He was it!" Tipp said in protest.

"Too late," Dickie said. "You're it." He tagged Tipp.

They continued to play tag and various other chase games until they were called in for lunch. They had to go wash up first, as they had gotten sweaty and dirty from all of the running and chasing.

They had their lunch on the deck overlooking the river. It was peaceful and serene. A pleasant departure from the excitement of the past few days. After they had finished with lunch, and conversation had dwindled, the topic of the children returning to their own time was brought up.

"We should return you home," Tesla said. "It's only right."

"We want to go home, but," Elina stopped short.

"But, what?"

"But, we will miss you all, and we'll never see you again," Elina said.

"Yes, there is that," Tesla admitted. "But, in truth, you would have never met any of us in the first place, so your experience here is an extraordinary thing, something for which you should be grateful." It was a reasonable way to view their journey.

"We need to go back," Tipp said. "Nikola's right."

"When do we go?" Elina asked.

"As soon as you're ready," Nikola said.

"Well, we need to say goodbye," Elina said. She went over to David and gave him a hug, and then to Harriet. Tipp followed her. Next she moved on to Tesla. He awkwardly hugged her back. Tipp chose to shake the inventor's hand instead. He seemed much more comfortable with this.

Finally the children came to Dickie. They both hugged him at once. All of them started to cry. It was as if they had been life long friends. They knew this was the last they would see of him, and that in their own time he was dead. It was like he was dying all over again.

"I won't let you down," Dickie said through tears. "I will make sure everything is there for you. I promise." They hugged him again, tears streaming down their faces.

"You're the two best friends I could have ever wished for."

"You, too," Tipp said.

"You're the best friend and great-grandfather, we could have ever had," Elina said through tears. "We're going to miss you."

Tipp and Elina stepped back from Dickie and held hands. Neither of them could remember the last time they had held hands willingly. Dickie hugged his mother.

"Okay," Elina said. "We're ready."

"I just need to know the date and time you're returning to," Tesla said.

"Uh, June 6th, 2013. It was night time, like 8pm," Tipp said.

"That sound about right," Elina said.

Tesla took his handheld device and made some adjustments on it. He pressed the two buttons simultaneously and it began to hum and crackle with energy. Blue and white electricity jumped and sparked from it and a sudden flash of light shot out, opening a portal in midair.

"Godspeed, Cavalier children," Tesla said.

"Goodbye, everybody," Tipp said.

"Goodbye," Elina said.

Tipp and Elina jumped through the Tesla portal.

CHAPTER 22

"Tipp! Elina!"

It was the first sound they heard as they hit the ground. They were outside the house, and the wind was blowing. It was dark. Their eyes were still adjusting from the bright flash of the Tesla portal. The telltale full body tingle assaulted their flesh from having gone through the portal. No matter how many times they went through it, they could not get used to the feeling. Like an arm that fell asleep from laying on it for too long, only all over their entire bodies. Eyelids and tongues, toes and earlobes. After a few moments the feeling subsided.

"Tipp! Elina!" The call came to them again. It was Sullo! They were back in 2013!

"Here! We're over here!" Elina yelled. She tried to stand, but Tipp was on top of her. He rolled off and allowed her to stand. He finally stood up as well, a little wobbly, but slowly becoming more stable. They could see a pair of flashlight beams moving around near the house. The beams grew closer to them.

As far as they could tell, they had come through the portal roughly in the same location as where they had been in 1933. There was no longer a deck here, though.

There was just an embankment that rolled down towards the river. They had tumbled down that embankment a bit, entangled with one another.

"We're here, Sullo!" Elina called.

"Elina!" Sullo raced to them and scooped them up. He hugged them both and they hugged him back. "Where have you two been? We looked all over the house for you!"

"Well, we, uh" Tipp started to tell him, but how could you tell someone that you had been time traveling for weeks?

"Never mind. We need to get to safety," Jeremiah Conklin said.

"Children, this is Jeremiah Conklin, he's with the FBI and a friend of your father's," Sullo said.

"Jeremiah!" Tipp said. "What are you doing here?"

"Your parents were kidnapped in the same way that your grandparents were. We fear that there are evil forces at work here. Our investigation has led us to believe that there may be an attempt on your lives," Conklin said.

A deep, pulsing noise could be heard in the distance. It grew louder and louder. It soon became obvious that the pulsing noise was the sound of helicopter blades.

"Are those your people?" Sullo asked. A wind began to pick up. It felt like a storm was beginning to blow in.

"No," Conklin said. "Even though Fort Drum is up here, we weren't authorized to request assistance. I didn't think it would be necessary. It does sound like they are headed this way, though. We need to find someplace to hide, fast."

"The basement," Sullo said. Distant thunder rumbled, even as the sounds of the rotor blades increased. The sky suddenly lit up as lightning struck out over the lake.

"No!" Tipp said. "I have another idea! Great Grandpa Dickie showed us. Come on!"

Tipp ran through the forest, even as the sound of the helicopters grew louder and louder. It was difficult to tell direction in the dark, and Tipp and Elina lost their way several times, but they corrected and found the right direction again. It was strange following the same path they had just taken while playing tag with a young Dickie not two hours earlier. The same ground was beneath their feet, it was just eight decades later. Were humans really meant to be that temporary?

The wind was really starting to howl now, and the trees were blowing back and forth. Another flash of lightning. This time it was much closer. The storm was rapidly approaching. Soon it would be raining.

Tipp led them through the trees, as he had a better sense of direction than his sister, and the rest followed. The helicopters grew closer even as the storm approached from the other direction. The four of them came into the clearing just as the helicopters came over the island. Spot lights shown down on the house, and they could see the debris that was being whipped up from the down draft of the helicopter blades. The helicopters circled the entire house, shining their lights into the windows and around the grounds.

"Who are they?" Tipp yelled over the noise.

"Bad people," Conklin said.

"What do they want," Elina asked.

"You!" Conklin yelled.

None of them expected what happened next. They weren't just helicopters, they were gunships. Through the trees, great orange balls of fire burst into the night air as the helicopters unleashed air to ground missiles into the mansion. They saw the light moments before they heard the explosion. The branches of the trees were whipped by the force of the rapidly expanding air.

"Go! Go! Go!" Conklin yelled over the noise of the explosions.

Suddenly the sky opened up with lightning and rain came down from the heavens. It took only seconds for them to be soaked. The flashes of lightning back lit the helicopters, and Tipp stole a glance as they ran across the clearing towards the door.

They didn't look like any helicopters he had ever seen. They looked more like huge airplanes with stubby wings, hovering over the ground. Every so often a bolt of lightning would jump up from the ground to one of the aircraft. Just then, they let loose another barrage of weapons fire.

The group reached the door in the wall just as a second explosion lit up the night sky. Tipp punched in the code.

One. Eight. Nine. One. The door slid open and they piled inside as a third explosion rocked the island.

"Wait!" Elina cried. "Where's Alonzo!"

"Who?" Sullo asked.

"Alonzo, the chef!" Elina said. "He's been Great Grandpa Dickie's Chef since 1967!"

"We don't have a chef!" Sullo said. Elina scowled with confusion. She sat with Alonzo and heard his life story over a sandwich before they had gone through the machine. It didn't make any sense!

After the doors closed off the noise from outside, they found themselves in a small, dimly lit room. It took a moment for them to realize that it wasn't a room at all, but an elevator. A metallic panel on the wall by the door held merely two options, up and down. Tipp reached over and hit the down button. The elevator came to life and it took them down. To what, they did not know. The floor shook beneath them as another explosion occurred outside. As they descended, the explosions proved to cause less and less of an impact. Finally the elevator stopped and the doors opened.

It was dark and cavernous, but warm.

"Stay here," Conklin said. He had his gun out and he slowly stepped forward into the darkness. Lights came on automatically and made everyone jump with surprise. It took a moment for the sight to register. What they saw was, what looked like, very comfortable living quarters. It was a well furnished, survival shelter.

"Woo Hoo!" The children yelled as they ran into the living quarters.

There were sleeping quarters, bathrooms, a well stocked galley, a game room which had a pool table and foosball table, a sauna, steam room and hot tub, an entertainment room with sofa and recliners and of course, video games. The children ran through the quarters exploring all of the rooms.

"Five bedrooms!" Tipp yelled.

"Three bathrooms!" Elina called out.

"Steam room, it's got a steam room. And a hot tub!" Tipp said. Elina was in the galley now, looking through the refrigerator and freezer. Then she was into the pantry.

"We've got food to last months, maybe years."

"As far as I can tell," Sullo said to Conklin. "We're fifty feet below the surface in solid granite. There's nothing short of a nuclear warhead that's going to get us in here. And even then it might take two or three of them."

"Good old Dickie," Tipp said with a smile as he ran back into the living room. "He did take care of us, didn't he. All the bedrooms have flat screen TVs." It wasn't just a well furnished survival shelter, it was what one might call a luxury suite. It had all of the comforts one might have if they were going to spend an extended stay at a resort or spa. It was as if Dickie had thought of everything. He had been true to his word all those years ago.

The living room area had a large screen television as well, with an array of Bluray movies and video game systems. Tipp flopped down on the over stuffed couch, picked up a controller and held it up to his cheek.

"Oh, how I've missed you most of all," he said.

"You act like you haven't played video games in weeks," Sullo said to him.

"Have we got a story for you," Elina said.

"Well, we're not going anywhere for awhile," Jeremiah replied. "Why don't you tell us."

Elina looked over at Tipp.

"Go ahead," Tipp said. "They're not going to believe you, anyway."

"Not going to believe what?" Sullo asked.

She told them.

It took nearly three hours to get through the bulk of the story. Tipp didn't interrupt once. He was so engrossed in his video games that she didn't really need to worry about that. Sullo and Jeremiah listened intently. Jeremiah even took out his digital notebook and scribbled down notes.

When she was done, they all leaned back and took a breath. Sullo cleared his throat and dabbed a bit of perspiration from his brow.

"I need a drink, anyone else want anything? I'm going to see what the refrigerator in this place has for us," he said getting up and walking towards the galley.

"I have to say, Elina. That's quite a story," Conklin said.

"Most people would have trouble believing it."

"Do you believe it?" Elina asked. Sullo returned with several cans of soda. He took one over to Tipp who paused the game so he could take a few sips.

"We both do," Sullo said.

"You do?" Elina asked with surprise.

"You do?" Tipp swiveled around on the sofa. "Why?"

"The Cavalier family and several other families around the world are still members of the great Resistance. The very same Resistance that overthrew the Emperor back in 1933. That struggle continues," Sullo said.

"My family is also part of that struggle," Conklin said. "I didn't know Sullivan and I were on the same side until I met him. But I recognized him the moment I pulled up to the dock. We think that the people who captured your parents and grandparents are part of an organization that has roots which stretch back to the Emperor's government. They call themselves "The Disciples". They are all over the world. They are in businesses and governments including our own. They wield influence all over. It looks like the Cavalier family is now in their crosshairs."

"Why?" Elina asked.

"It would seem," Sullo said. "Because you were at the center of the operation that brought down the Emperor. Maybe it's revenge. Maybe the Emperor's demise hinged on the two of you using Tesla's machine and going back in time. Think about it, do you remember in your history studies anything about the Emperor, or The Resistance movement?"

"No," Elina said. "I don't remember that at all."

"Nope," Tipp echoed

"See," Sullo replied. "It's part of the required curriculum. You most certainly would have been told of the struggle, the overthrow of the mechanized army, the reinstitution of the constitution and restoration of the constitutional republic. My guess is that by going back in time, you shifted the time line and now The Disciples are going to come after you."

"They are going to come after us," Conklin corrected. "We're not going to let anything happen to you. The Disciples are not stronger than the descendants of the sworn brothers of The Resistance. We will find your parents and grandparents and make sure you are safe."

"How long do we have to stay down here?" Elina asked.

"As long as we have to," Conklin said.

The Cavalier family will return in
THE TESLA RESISTANCE

Acknowledgments

I would first like to thank my wonderful wife Belinda and my three children for supporting me through all those afternoons and evenings when I needed to disappear to write and edit. I hope it was worth it. I'd also like to thank my brothers who aided me in my last minute scramble to meet deadline. Thanks, bros. Lastly, I'd like to thank my English teachers from Chenango Valley Schools who gave me the foundation I needed to even believe I could start writing. I hope you never get your hands on this book and see how much I've forgotten about proper English!

About the Author

Adam Cornell was born in upstate New York but spent some of his life in Louisiana, which he considers his second home. He began writing in grade school and could never kick the habit. He has previously written a screenplay and television pilot, both of which never got past the first stages of production. Adam has previously worked on the air as a radio personality utilizing the name Adam Speed while in Baton Rouge and New Orleans, LA as well as Elmira, NY. He has also made a career in the field of graphic design, working at several ad agencies along with other companies in the printing, housewares and automotive industries. Adam currently lives with his wife and three children in Watertown, NY.

Made in the USA
San Bernardino, CA
21 January 2019